Death Elements

Wendy Cartmell

Costa Press

Praise for Wendy Cartmell
'A pretty extraordinary talent' –
Best Selling Crime Thrillers
'This is genre fiction at its best, suspense that rivets
and a mystery that keeps you guessing.' –
A R Symmonds on Goodreads

.

As Oscar Wilde put it
"All men kill the thing they love."

Asphyxiophilia
Asphyxiation or breath control play,
is the intentional restriction of oxygen to the brain
for the purpose of sexual arousal.

The papers call him the Choker. Crane and
Anderson call him a sadomasochist. But whatever his
name is, the Major Crimes team have to find him. And
fast. Because time is running out. It won't be long
before he kills again.

Boy

You'd be surprised how still I can sit. I'm doing it now. My bottom is on the floor, my knees are pulled up and my arms wrapped around them. I'm watching a spider. A big, black, fat one. He's just behind that rock. He came out once, but I frightened him by moving, so he ran away and I had to start over. I won't make that mistake again. I can wait for ages and ages.

Here he comes. I can see one black leg poking out. Here comes another and another. A spider has eight legs. I learned that at school. I like school, it's interesting. I'm not like some of the other children. They mess about, don't concentrate and don't try their hardest. I always try my hardest. Daddy makes sure of that. Daddy helped me to learn to sit still. He said I was a terrible wriggler, so he tied me to a chair until I stopped. He doesn't have to tie me down anymore. I can sit still for ages, until he tells me I can get down. It makes me feel funny inside. I quite like that feeling. So I do as I'm told.

I can see the spider's body now. He's inching his way out from his hiding place, his legs reaching out ahead of him, making sure there's nothing in his way. And there isn't. Not really. Only my little hand and if I keep it still enough he'll crawl right onto it.

The spider is climbing onto my hand now. One leg, two. He's an old slow coach but I can wait. Nearly there…

My fingers curl over his body, trapping him inside my hand. Got him!

I hold the spider's body between my finger and thumb, leaving his legs dangling in the air. Now I can count them. The first leg comes off easily, making him wriggle even more. He isn't as good as being still as I am. As I pull off each leg I sing quietly to myself…

Incy wincy spider…

Aldershot Mail Online

Local Murder

An unknown male is being sought by police, after a body was found yesterday in an apartment in Aldershot. The woman, yet to be positively identified, is thought to have been found tied to the bed, with a silk scarf around her neck. Due to the apparent sexual nature of the crime, police believe she could have been partaking in a sex game. They are awaiting the results of the post mortem, which will take place today, but the working theory is that she was choked to death with the colourful silk scarf that was found wound around her neck.

We believe Aldershot Police will be holding a press conference later today, when they hope to release the name of the victim, and the results of the post mortem. At that time, we hope to find out if they have any leads as to the identity of this mysterious choker.

Crane

"A mysterious choker!" snorted Anderson as he threw his tablet across the table and ran his hand over his hair, trying to tame the wisps of grey that should have covered his bald spot, but never did.

Crane winced and caught it just as it teetered on the edge. "Careful, Derek," he admonished. "Your tablet isn't as robust as the files of paper you normally chuck around. You need to be more careful with the technology we've been given, otherwise all your budget will be taken up with repairs and replacements."

"Well!" Anderson glared at Crane, in an amusing role reversal of their emotional traits, at least amusing in Crane's eyes.

But he was careful not to smile. DI Derek Anderson of the Hampshire Police Major Crimes Team (effectively his boss) seemed to be acting more like his civilian consultant (Sgt Major Crane Retired ex-army SIB investigator) in his anger and mannerisms. The current focus of his derision was the latest article by the new editor of the Aldershot News, Diane Cambers. Online - the day after they had found the dead girl and when no formal announcement had been made about the murder.

"She is obviously taking full advantage of modern communication methods, now she's editor," Crane said, indicating the home page of the Aldershot News On-Line.

"Yes, but who is her source?" Anderson looked through the office window at the rest of his team. "We didn't release the information that a silk scarf was found around her neck, nor that we thought it could be a sex-game gone wrong."

"It could be anyone, Derek. It's not necessarily one of ours, but it could be any neighbour, paramedic, or member of the hospital staff, including the morgue assistants."

It still seemed strange to Crane, to think of the civilian police as 'one of ours'. After nearly twenty-two years in the British Army it had taken quite a while for the adjustment in his circumstances to begin to appear normal.

"Yeah, alright, I get it. The possibilities are endless."

"Exactly." Crane pulled up the cuff of his white shirt and glanced at his watch. "Anyway, are you ready for the off?"

"What?" Anderson seemed momentarily confused. "Oh, right, the autopsy." He stood and began to collect his things, stuffing his phone and his keys into the pocket of his tweed jacket. "Not that we really need to go, Diane Chambers seems to have all the facts at her finger tips," he grumbled. "I'm sure we can read all about the post mortem online later."

"Oh cheer up," Crane said, grabbing his stick and levering himself up from his chair. "Look, the sun is shining; it's a beautiful day…"

"And we're going to spend the rest of it watching Major Martin slice up a beautiful young girl who didn't deserve to die."

"Well, when you put it that way."

"I do," said Derek, pulling open the office door. "I do."

"So, is it true then, boss?" DC Ciaran Douglas addressed both men as Crane and Anderson arrived back at Aldershot Police Station from their visit to Frimley Park Hospital.

"Is what true?" Crane asked, although he suspected he knew full well what Douglas was talking about.

"That she was killed by being choked to death during sex? What did Major Martin say?"

"Just in case it was a sex-game related death, I've been looking up asphyxiophilia, guv," Holly their computer analyst butted in. "I'm collecting lots of background information for you."

"Oh, joy," was Derek's response. "Get the coffees in, Ciaran, and we'll talk about it in my office."

Since the formation of a major crimes team, consisting of DI Anderson, Tom Crane, DC Ciaran Douglas and computer expert Holly Abbott, Anderson had been allocated a larger office, which was big enough to contain a conference table and, at Crane's insistence, a large white board all along one wall. Douglas and Holly sat outside at desks facing each other. Holly's was crammed with various pieces of technical equipment Crane neither knew the names of, nor understood how they worked. Crane himself had a desk on the other side of Anderson's door. He still wasn't used to not having an office of his own and as a result spent far more time in Anderson's than he really should do.

Holly Abbott, a computer sciences graduate, had

joined the police, as she put it, 'to put her skills to good use, rather than helping capitalists make even more money than they already had, or by developing new products people couldn't live without and paid an absolute fortune for'. Crane definitely got that point of view, having a young son who was growing up fast and would inevitably want the latest devices before long. Her brown shoulder length hair was pulled into two plaits. Nothing strange about that. But when you added a startling blue fringe and pink sides, it started to look rather avant-garde. Her long sleeved tee-shirt in muddy green matched the colour of her many-pocketed cargo pants. She was painfully thin and rather studious in her large black framed glasses. She never drank coffee, only green tea, or some blended mush or other that sat in the fridge quietly fermenting.

DC Ciaran Douglas, quite trendy in his slim trousers and knitted ties, which mostly never matched his shirt, was a police graduate on a fast track career path. Aged in his mid-twenties, he looked younger, at least to Crane and Anderson. Bringing to the party the new policing methods and being fresh out of Hendon, Douglas now needed on the job experience.

Crane had to acknowledge he and Anderson were dinosaurs by comparison to the two bright young things, but as a team, the four complimented each other. Age and experience versus the brave new world and technologically savvy younger members.

By the time Douglas came in balancing a tray with four mugs on it, Anderson indicated to Crane that he should start the briefing.

Dressed in his usual work uniform of black suit and white shirt and leaning on his stick, courtesy of the injury that had invalided him out of the British Army, he began,

"Well, Major Martin, our friendly local medical examiner, is definitely floating the idea of asphyxiophilia being the main contributor to Sally Sawyer's death."

"Told you," grinned Holly.

"But it wasn't the cause?" Douglas frowned.

"No, death was due to a massive heart attack. As her heart was completely healthy and she had no other underlying medical problems, he feels the evidence he found showing starvation of oxygen to her brain, caused by pressure being put on her carotid arteries, led to a heart attack. There were faint bruises on her neck from thumbs and indication that the scarf we found wound around her neck, had been pulled tight. He thinks the silk scarf was used to ensure maximum potency and least bruising."

"Was it consensual?"

"Probably, as there was no other bruising found, nor injuries. There was minimal bruising from the restraints. If she'd been tied up against her will, the Major says there were would more in the way of abrasions."

"Jesus," muttered Holly, chewing one end of her platted hair.

Crane indicated the photographs he'd put up on the white board of Sally lying dead on her bed.

"As we saw from the crime scene, the bed linen had been removed and was found in the washing machine. There was an overall smell of bleach in the flat and the Major has confirmed her body was washed down with the stuff. Presumably that was all done by the perpetrator. Sally's flat mate, Donna, didn't do it and the smell of bleach was particularly strong when she arrived back home yesterday and found her friend's body."

"And there's no forensic evidence on her at all?" asked Douglas.

"No, none. Not after all that bleach."

"No semen?"

"No, Ciaran, only faint traces of a lubricant commonly used on condoms."

"He really made sure there was nothing of himself left in the flat," said Anderson. "Right down to dousing the scarves he'd used in a solution of bleach as well."

"Or her, sir," said Holly and they all turned and gaped at her. "Our killer could equally be a woman. It's not just blokes that enjoy BDSM, you know," she said.

"I suppose you're right," said Crane, a slight flush creeping up his face.

BBC NEWS

"This is the BBC Local News at six-thirty with Ingrid Strange. Our top story this evening. A young woman found dead two days ago in a flat in Aldershot, Hampshire, has been identified as Sally Sawyer, aged 24. A single girl, she shared a flat with a friend, who has declined to be interviewed. Neighbours of Sally have described her death as 'tragic' and 'unbelievable'.

"We can now cross to our correspondent, Carol Walker, who is near to the flat where Sally lived. What more can you tell us, Carol?"

"Thank you, Ingrid. Well, as you can see, I'm about 100 yards away from the block of flats where Sally lived and standing by the police cordon. The whole community is in shock. I have with me Gloria Simms, a near neighbour. Thank you for talking to us, Ms Simms. What was Sally like?"

"She was a wonderful, caring, young woman. I just can't believe she's gone!"

"Did you know her well?"

"Oh, oh, just to say hello to…. but I saw her most mornings and she always had a smile on her face!"

"Thank you, Ms Simms. Well, Ingrid, the police have issued a statement which says they are doing everything they can to bring Sally's killer to justice and that her family have asked for privacy

at this most difficult time. I do know the police have been conducting house to house enquiries in the vicinity of her apartment."

"Is there anything more on the manner of her death, now an autopsy has been completed?"

"Well there have been rumours that some sort of sex-game was involved, and as she was found with a colourful silk scarf around her neck, the current thinking is that possibly 'breath control play' was a factor in her death. This is the intentional restriction of oxygen to the brain for the purpose of sexual arousal. Some people find reducing or severing air flow via strangulation or suffocation can heighten sexual arousal and orgasmic pleasure. Colloquially, a person engaging in this activity is sometimes called a 'gasper' and is the submissive. The 'choker' takes the more dominant role, which is why some newspapers have been calling the killer, The Choker."

"Can you tell me what charges the perpetrator is likely to face?"

"That's a good question, Carol. I talked to the police about that and they said it depended upon the killer's intention. If it was accidental, then a charge of manslaughter would be brought, but if it was intentional, it would be a clear case of murder. In the meantime, the mound of flowers left at the entrance to the apartment block where Sally lived, continues to grow and there is talk of a silent candlelight vigil to be held this evening. Back to you in the studio, Ingrid."

"Thank you, Carol. And now on to other news…"

Theresa

Theresa snapped off the television with the remote control when the item had finished. That poor girl, she thought, being killed for someone's sexual gratification. What was the world coming to? She wasn't exactly a prude; she was sure she liked sex as much as the next person. But to be strangled whilst having it? The thought made her shudder and her hands went instinctively to her neck.

He'd tried that once, her husband Tim, but she'd hated it. She'd thought it disgusting, depraved and very dangerous. She was clearly right, in the light of what had just happened.

They'd had a huge row about it at the time and he'd promised never to do anything like that to her again. But she still flinched every time his hand went anywhere near her exposed neck. She had never told anyone about the awful incident and had worn a scarf for a week afterwards until the bruises faded. She'd got some funny looks, but when anyone enquired, she'd managed to mumble something about having a sore throat and wanting to keep it warm.

Getting off the settee, she wandered to the window

and looked out, the net curtain twitching, but all she could see was her own face reflected back at her, giving her a glimpse of how she might look in old age. Her long hair was bleached grey, her eyes dulled by worry and a slight flaw in the glass made her mouth, chin and neck distorted with wrinkles. Turning away from the depressing image she wondered how many men would want that type of sex? She smoothed her neck, this time to dispel the wrinkles she'd see in her reflection. Mr Jones across the street? Kevin and Clive, the gay couple next door? Her two sons, now grown men? No surely not, the very thought was preposterous.

Leaving the window, she wandered the house, putting an ornament straight here, smoothing the curtains there. There was no cleaning to be done. She'd finished it all that morning, with the usual programmes on the television for company. She alternated between BBC and ITV. She liked This Morning but it got a bit silly at times, so then she turned over and watched Homes Under the Hammer, returning to ITV for Loose Women.

Looking at her watch she could see it was only seven o'clock and the empty night stretched before her. Tim was away, holed up in a hotel somewhere, no doubt in his room drinking the mini bar dry, or downstairs laughing and chatting with his fellow academics. She'd never been as clever as her husband and because she'd been a stay at home mum she'd been left with no real skills, now their two children had grown up and left home. In the past she'd tried charity work but found the other women to be self-absorbed bitches, more concerned with themselves than the charities they were supposed to be helping. Lately she'd been applying for jobs, but hadn't yet got an interview, no doubt because of her age and lack of experience. Helping out in the Red

Cross charity shop obviously wasn't sufficient for today's picky employers.

Feeling lonely, she reached for the phone to call someone. Anyone. She tried Tim, but his phone was switched off. Neither of her sons answered, the calls just ringing and ringing until she gave up. So much for her husband and sons keeping her company.

She could call a friend, she supposed. But thinking about it, she wasn't actually sure that she had any. None that she could call about the disquiet that was settling over her, at any rate. Not Jo from next door, nor Kevin and Clive on the other side. No, this was far too personal a problem rattling around in her brain.

She finished her tour of the house and put the television back on, just for background noise more than anything. Company. It was still on the news channel and so once again she heard the story of Sally who had been killed in Aldershot.

She stilled with the TV remote in her hand. Aldershot? It couldn't be. No, it wasn't possible. Was it? She moved over to the bureau, a relic from her parents she had been too sentimental to discard and opening the lid, she rummaged in the drawers. She was sure she'd put the details of Tim's conference in there somewhere. Yes, there it was.

Opening the envelope, she looked at the picture of the hotel on the front of the glossy brochure. The Mount – a country house hotel for the discerning client, it described itself as. Set in beautiful countryside, near to the towns of Aldershot and Farnborough.

The brochure fluttered to the floor and her hands went to her neck again.

That poor girl.

Was it possible that her husband, Tim Dennison,

Professor of Criminology at Reading University, had a dark secret only she knew about? If so, was it a secret he'd kill to keep?

Ciaran

Donna Price opened the hotel room door in response to his knock, far quicker than he thought she would.

"Donna Price? I'm DC Ciaran Douglas, Hampshire Police." As she looked confused he continued, "I'd like a word with you about your flat mate Sally. I've just got a few follow up questions."

"Oh, sorry, you weren't who I was expecting. I'm waiting for a taxi to take me to the airport." She indicated the hand luggage sized case she was holding.

She wasn't what he was expecting either. The girl's make up was perfect, at least to Ciaran's eyes. But then what did he know, being a bloke? All he knew was she looked beautiful; poised, polished, and every bit the air hostess she was. Her short dark pixie haircut suited her and her fitted blue uniform emphasised her slim figure. She explained he'd just caught her as she was soon to leave her hotel, ready to go to Heathrow to board a long haul flight to Australia. She invited him in and they stood rather awkwardly in the space at the end of the twin beds and between the dresser.

"Um, had you known Sally long?" Ciaran managed to blurt out, studying her shoes instead of that amazing face, in his embarrassment.

"I didn't know her at all before she moved in," said Donna. "That was about three years ago," she added, as if anticipating his next question.

"Did you get on well?"

"Of course, otherwise she wouldn't have stayed that long. The flat is mine, you see, she is, was, my lodger." Her eyes filled with tears. "And she became a friend." Donna wiped under each eye with her finger and blinked.

"What about a boyfriend? Was there anyone special in her life?"

Donna sat on the bed and shook her head slightly. "No, not that I know of. There were men she saw and she told me about them occasionally. But no 'significant other' if you know what I mean."

Ciaran nodded, but he wasn't at all sure he did know what she meant. He'd never been anyone's 'significant other' as far as he knew.

"Was she a member of any dating sites? That's how most people meet these days."

"Oh, so you have experience of that, do you?" Donna smiled and Ciaran blushed at the teasing remark.

He was very much afraid she was getting the upper hand in this interview and it wasn't supposed to be like that. So, after clearing his throat, he said in what he hoped was a solemn tone, "Please, Donna, this is really important."

"Sorry," she said and smiled a little. "I didn't mean to trivialise what's happened. But no, I don't know if she was on any dating sites. There are so many of them around these days, including the phone app thingy that tells you when someone you might like is near to your location and the ones where you have to skim through faces." She picked at bits of fluff on her skirt.

"But you don't know if she had signed up to any?"

"No, sorry, she never mentioned it. You'll have to check her phone and laptop."

"We would if we could find them. Do you know what devices she had?"

"Sure, an iPhone and a MacBook. I think both of them were pretty old, but they worked well enough. Sally always said there was no point in upgrading them just so you could show them off and pretend like you had loads of money."

He thought about the brand new Samsung S6 Edge mobile phone he had in his pocket and had been desperate to upgrade to, and kept his opinion to himself.

"Can you just write down any mobile numbers you have for her and also any email addresses?" he asked and handed her his notebook.

"Didn't you find those from papers and stuff in her room?"

"We found a mobile phone bill, but email addresses aren't necessarily logged anywhere and she could have had a pre-paid mobile we know nothing about."

"Oh, right, yes, of course," she mumbled and scribbled away. Handing the notebook back she said, "I know this sounds awful, but do you know when I'll be able to move back in?"

"I'm afraid your flat is still a crime scene. It could be a week or so yet. Perhaps you could give me a ring when you get back?" he said and handed her his card.

"Thanks," she grinned as she took it. "I'll make sure I do that."

Ciaran once again felt an irritating blush begin to form and to hide his embarrassment he messed about with putting his notebook away in his coat pocket. "If you think of anything that might help us in the meantime, please phone or send a message."

"Of course I will, but to be honest I'm trying not to think about it. I've lost a good friend, who died in my flat and I've got to come to terms with living there without her and with knowing what happened in her bedroom. And I've got to keep it together enough to go to work and pretend like nothing happened while I'm there."

"I'm sorry… " Ciaran didn't know what else to say. They didn't teach you at Hendon how to deal with an upset, beautiful young woman, who he wanted to put his arms around and comfort. "If you need someone to talk to you can always, well, you know…"

That brought a teary smile. "I know," she said. "Thanks."

"Well, I better…"

"Yes, you had…"

"Um, bye," he managed to mutter before fleeing the room, berating himself for making a complete balls up of the interview. The only saving grace being neither Crane nor Anderson were around to witness it, nor was Holly. Which reminded him, he had to tell her about the devices when he got back to the office. Perhaps she could try and trace them or something.

Theresa

The next morning the murder of Sally Sawyer was still all over the news. But this time there was a phone number to call. An anonymous tip line or something. It seemed every time Theresa walked past the screen, the murder was the top story and the phone number was flashing. Pulling her eye towards it. Filling the screen so it couldn't be ignored.

Walking into the kitchen she began to clear away her breakfast things, but over the clattering of the crockery, the TV could still be heard. On and on the news item went; what a wonderful girl she was, how it was a crying shame, a life snuffed out too soon. The platitudes for Sally went on and on until she ran back into the living room and turned the bloody thing off.

Silence filled the space, but whilst one voice had been stopped, another took its place. *It could be him*, it whispered in her head. *You know it could. What are you going to do about it? You need to tell someone.*

"But I don't know anything," she yelled at the empty room, but her words were absorbed by the soft furnishings. "There's nothing I can do!" The curtains moved as though disturbed by her shouting.

What if it is him? the voice started up again. *How many more girls have to die before you do the right thing?*

She stomped up the stairs, hoping making the bed and cleaning the bathroom would stop the calls for her to act. In the bedroom she became calmer, shaking out the duvet and plumping the pillows. The room was a bit stuffy, so she opened the window which looked out onto the back garden. Leaning out and taking deep breaths of fresh air, she began to feel better.

She watched a blackbird hop across the grass, which was as green and smooth as a bowling green. It was one of Tim's hobbies, the back lawn. The bird stopped, did a little dance as he tapped the ground and was rewarded with a worm. She smiled indulgently at it. Maybe he felt her presence at the window, for he turned his beady eyes on her and opening his mouth, dropped the worm onto the grass.

You know what to do, he chirped. *Do the right thing. Don't let anyone else die.*

By now she was convinced she was a forty-something, lonely housewife, going mad with boredom and withdrawing her head, she slammed the window shut. But she wasn't quick enough, as she heard the trees rustled and sigh, *Make the call, make the call.*

"Alright, alright! I'll do what you want, just leave me alone!"

Sobbing and stumbling down the stairs, she reached for the phone, but couldn't remember the number to call. Grabbing the remote and turning the TV back on, she saw the number was still on the screen. 0800 111 222. With trembling fingers she keyed in the digits and was rewarded with the sound of ringing.

"Crime Stoppers, how may I help you?" the male operator sounded much calmer than she was.

"I…" Teresa's mouth was dry and she licked her cracked lips. "I…" she tried again. Close to tears she bunched her free hand into a fist, dug her fingernails into her palms and blurted out, "I think I know who killed Sally Sawyer."

By tea time, no one had rung her back. Theresa had left her mobile number, her name and her husband's name. But they still hadn't called as she finished the final preparations for dinner later that afternoon. She checked her mobile for what felt like the hundredth time that day and there was still no missed call from the police. Actually no missed calls, or answered calls, from anyone. She'd spent most of the day pacing the house and the garden and then taking a turn around the block, to try and still her shaking hands and clear her head.

Normally she would have gone into town, perhaps chosen some new books from the library and stopped for a coffee and a cake. But looking in the mirror that morning, and seeing someone who looked more like a mad woman than a respectable middle-class wife, she'd stayed at home and tried to do something with her appearance instead.

So now she was showered, dressed casually in trousers and a shirt and her hair, freshly washed, was gleaming, just the way she liked it. The wrong side of forty - she'd had their first child at eighteen - she often wondered if she should cut her hair in line with her advancing years. But in many ways her tresses were her best feature and she felt she would easily disappear into the wallpaper without them. For everything else about her screamed mumsy. Some would say she was the classic English rose with her pale skin, clear blue eyes and dark hair. But she knew she was pear-shaped; too wide at the hips and hadn't much in the way of breasts.

She'd become pregnant after they'd met in their first year at the local university. But Tim had stood by her and married her, so she'd done her best to support him as he graduated with a First Class Honours Degree, did a Master's degree and then courtesy of a PhD, entered the hallowed halls of academia. But all the while she had pushed her own academic yearnings to the back of her mind. Family came first. Always. Her parents had taught her that. And Tim had agreed with them. When she'd found out she was pregnant she'd considered an abortion, as she was loving learning and university life, but no one else had agreed with her. 'That would be a terrible thing to do,' she was told. 'How could you ever contemplate something like that?' they'd asked. But in the back of her mind, Theresa had always resented the fact that Tim had carried on with his life the way he'd envisaged it and she hadn't been able to. Not that she didn't love her boys. Of course she did. Who wouldn't? The thing was, no one else seemed to appreciate how much she'd given up to have them.

Then there was the matter of further education. For years she'd harboured a desire to complete her degree. If nothing else, surely she would have been able to attend university as a mature student once the children were old enough. But that had been frowned upon also. Once more she was faced with the negative pressure her parents and Tim were so good at. 'Why would you want to do that?' she'd been asked. 'Surely it's not necessary? You have a lovely family and a lovely home, what more could you want?' She could hear them now, the outrage, the disapproval clear in their words and tone.

She was peeling potatoes in the kitchen at the back of

the house when Tim arrived back home, interrupting her spiralling thoughts.

His, "Hello, love," made her drop the knife with a clatter into the sink.

"Jesus," she said, turning round and proffering her cheek for a kiss. "You gave me a fright. Good trip?" she asked and returned to her peeling.

"Oh, you know," he said.

She didn't know, of course, but let it pass. She was having enough trouble concentrating on not slicing her fingers open with the knife, without having to make conversation at the same time.

"How long's dinner?"

"About an hour."

"Great," he replied. "I'll grab a shower and unpack."

As he walked out of the room, she let go of the knife again and grabbed the edge of the sink, breathing deeply in and out, to try and still her fluttering heartbeat. After a while she managed to complete the dinner preparations.

Later, over dinner, he told her about his conference, appearing completely normal. He showed her the papers and brochures he'd brought back with him and talked about speakers she would have found interesting. And there was the rub, she supposed. Would have found interesting. If she hadn't given up everything for her family, only for them to leave her and move on with their lives, not caring that she was left behind, bereft.

Forcing such treacherous thoughts away, she gradually relaxed with the aid of a couple of glasses of wine. Tim's homecoming was no different from any other. She couldn't detect anything strange or different about him. They normally rubbed along fairly happily and had a well-worn routine, which they both unconsciously followed.

They took cups of tea through to the lounge, where they watched TV for an hour or so, before turning in for an early night. Within minutes Tim was fast asleep beside her, but it took her a while longer to drop off, as she fussed and fretted over the call she'd made to Crime Stoppers. She now hoped they wouldn't ring back. She wasn't sure about anything anymore. Pushing her hair off her face, she felt her cheeks burning with embarrassment in the dark.

Anderson

"Oy, come back here you little shit!" Anderson called to the scrawny kid holding a mobile phone, who had started running away from him the moment he identified himself as a policeman. "I only want the bloody phone, not you!" he called. But it made no difference; the lad was off down the street like Hussein Bolt.

Anderson grinned and walked after the boy, safe in the knowledge that Ciaran was at the other end of the alley, waiting with a police car and, sure enough, by the time Anderson got there, the lad was in the back, kicking effectually at the back of the driver's seat.

"Has he said anything?" Anderson asked as they climbed in the car.

"No. At least nothing that resembled the Queen's English and involved complete sentences."

"Got the phone?"

"Yeah," and Douglas held up an evidence bag with a mobile in it.

"Right you," Anderson said, turning in his seat to look at the young boy behind him. He couldn't have been much older than eleven or twelve years old and Anderson was saddened by the thought of a young life being wasted so early. What was wrong with kids today? He was buggered if he knew. "Where'd you get the phone?"

"Fuck off, pig!"

"Oh, come on, that's not going to get us anywhere, is it?"

But the boy refused to be placated and continued swearing.

The team had received a call from a community policeman telling him the word was out that the young lad in the car with them was the one to go to if you wanted a knocked-off mobile and his patch was the area of Aldershot where Sally Smith had lived. Fancying a bit of fresh air and because he missed being on the streets himself, he'd decided to take Ciaran with him and see what his young DC was made of.

"You try, Douglas."

Ciaran climbed out of the car, opened the back door and yanked the lad off the seat and out of the vehicle. Anderson joined him, looking forward to seeing what Douglas would do. Pushing him up against the bodywork, Douglas got in the boy's face and said, "Right, you little shit, you either tell me where you got the phone and then you can leave, or you can continue being a bloody idiot and spend a night in the cells."

"You can't touch me, I'm a minor!" the boy spat.

"Prove it. Show me some ID."

That made the boy pause before he said, "Ain't got none on me."

"Well then, I'll have to take you down the station and put you in a cell until I can verify who you are. Come on, get back in."

"Wait!"

Ciaran paused and Anderson smiled, pleased with his

young DC's performance so far.

"If I tell you what I know, I can go, yeah?"

"Yeah. But don't be spinning me any lies, or I'll be back for you."

"Well, I got it off a friend, didn't I? No bloody good anyway. Crappy old thing."

"And this friend's name?"

"Well, he's not really a friend, like. It was Bobby, the homeless lad who hangs around near the local shops."

"I know him. And where did Bobby get it?"

"Said he found it in the skip behind the newsagents."

"Did he have anything else for sale?"

"Nah, just that. Look you won't tell him it were me grassed him up, will ya?"

Ciaran pulled the boy around.

"I'll think about it. Now bugger off."

The boy didn't need telling twice and in an instant was around the corner and out of sight.

"Good work, lad," said Anderson, pleased Ciaran had elicited the information they needed. "Just one thing, why didn't you get his name?"

"No point, sir. I didn't think we needed it and it was a bit of reverse psychology as well. All the time he thought he was anonymous, the more comfortable he'd be with giving me information. If I'd have pushed for his name and address, he could have become as stubborn as a donkey and I wouldn't have got anything out of him."

Anderson liked the theory behind Ciaran's actions. He would have done the same, but by instinct, rather than being able to explain it in terms of psychology. As they climbed back into the car Anderson radioed for a couple of uniforms to go and check out the contents of the skip. There might still be something hidden there and he was damn sure it wasn't going to be him climbing in it to take a look. He also told them he wanted any CCTV footage, if there was any, from the newsagents.

When they arrived back at the station, Anderson passed the phone to Holly.

"What do you think? Can you get anything from it?"

"Well I'll be able to check if it was Sally's phone," she said. "But to be honest, guv, don't hold your breath, it's a pretty old model."

"Try your best," he said.

Holly looked askance. "Of course, guv. I never do anything other than my best."

Anderson didn't trust himself to reply, afraid he'd put his foot in it again, so just nodded and wandered off to find Crane. He was sure his young analyst was slightly autistic. She was just so bloody clever and so literal.

Boy

Daddy reads to me. He says I'm old enough to hear the fairy tales he was so fond of when he was a boy. But he says they're not the Disney versions, but the real ones. I don't quite know what that means, but I don't ask him. I always do as Daddy tells me.

He has just read Little Red Riding Hood to me and now I'm supposed to go to sleep. But I'm finding it very difficult. I keep thinking of the story. Of Little Red Riding Hood being abducted by the Wolf and him then climbing into bed with her.

I wonder what he did to her? I wonder how she would have felt? Would she have minded being abducted? The story doesn't say. Would the Wolf have tied her up? Would it be like when Daddy used to tie me to a chair?

I don't know, but it's making me feel funny inside again. It's that feeling I used to get when I was little. I'm growing up now. Daddy says I'm too old to be tied to a chair anymore. So if I'm bad he makes me sit in the cupboard under the stairs. I have to stay there until he says I can come out. I could open the door myself. It's not locked and there is a handle on the inside. But I never do. I like to be good. I like the feeling of being good.

Daddy has left the book for me to read myself. So I reach for it and my torch. Making a little tent with the duvet over my head and putting the torch, on I start to read.

What big teeth you've got… all the better to eat you with.

Theresa

Tim seemed distracted, walking around the house searching for his things and ignoring the cup of tea and the breakfast she'd laid out on the kitchen table.

"Tim!" Theresa called, "don't you want this breakfast?"

"What?" he popped his head around the kitchen door.

"Breakfast - do you want it?"

"Too much on, got to get to the university, lots of catching up to do after being away."

Following him into the hallway, where he was putting on his coat, she said, "I'll see you for dinner, then."

Tim froze, one arm in his coat and the other out. "Um, no, not tonight."

"Oh," Theresa said. She was sure last night he'd said he'd be home at the normal time the following evening.

"Yeah, I forgot about a visiting speaker tonight, something the Dean has arranged. You know what that means."

Theresa was only too aware of what it meant. Drinks, dinner and then finally a speech over coffee and brandy. The old boys' club at its finest. It was so bloody unfair.

Theresa's breath hitched and she had to quickly pull herself together before Tim noticed.

"Oh, anyone I know?" she asked, trying for nonchalance, but not quite making it and stuffing her hands in her dressing gown so their trembling wouldn't give her away.

"Doubt it. Don't wait up," he said and then he was out of the door as quickly as if a rabid dog were at his heels.

No kiss. No, 'have a nice day'. Nothing. She stood there, looking at the closed door, feeling foolish, undervalued and undermined. Any confidence she'd felt about being able to face the day seeped out of her eyes with her tears.

Walking back into the kitchen, she looked at the meal of boiled eggs and toast laid out on the kitchen table and the thought of eating it alone made her feel nauseous. She couldn't get over the unfeeling, dismissive way Tim had left the house. She grabbed a cup of coffee and turning her back on the pretty crockery and matching egg cups, went into the lounge to watch the television.

By mid-morning she was upstairs tidying up. On Tim's side of the bed she found briefing papers on the speaker he'd mentioned that morning. She knew Tim liked to be well prepared, always said that to appear knowledgeable to both the speaker and his colleagues, made him look good and placed him in good stead for any promotions, or interesting projects that might come along.

Sitting on the bed, she began to leaf through them, quickly becoming absorbed. Dr Craig Juniper was a renowned speaker on forensic practices, which fitted into the broader scope of Tim's subject, Criminology. On the one hand Teresa was glad Tim had left the information behind, for now they could have a discussion on the speech, maybe tomorrow. But on the other, she knew Tim would be concerned, thinking maybe he had lost the notes. What if he hadn't read them yet?

Picking up the phone resting on the bedside table, she rang Tim's mobile, but it wasn't answered. So she tried his secretary.

"Hi Rose," she said. "Theresa here. Look Tim's left his notes here on the visiting speaker tonight. Can you let him know? I can bring them over for him if he needs them."

"Speaker?"

"Yes, Dr Craig Juniper."

"Tonight?"

"Yes, Rose. What's the matter?" Theresa could hear the rustling of paper and the clicking of a computer keyboard in the background.

"Sorry, Theresa, but that's next week."

"Oh," Theresa stilled. She wanted to ask Rose if she was sure, but stopped the words before they flew out of her mouth. She knew Rose didn't make errors. Instead she said, "No worries, then, I must have made a mistake. Don't tell Tim I called, with you? Don't want him thinking I was worrying unnecessarily."

"That's okay…"

Theresa replaced the telephone, cutting off Rose's drivel and stumbled down the stairs and into the kitchen, where she sat in a chair. Lies. Tim's words that morning had been lies. All lies. What the hell was going on? With her head swimming and fighting the desire to close her eyes and collapse to the floor, Theresa managed to fill a glass with water and open the back door. Tumbling out into the garden, she sat down on the edge of the paving slabs of the patio, sipping the water and looking at the expanse of Tim's perfect lawn.

After a while she came to a decision and fished her mobile out of the pocket of her jeans and quickly making the call before she could change her mind. She'd looked up the number in a fit of pique earlier and had programmed it into her mobile.

"Aldershot Police Station."

The voice on the other end of the phone sounded gruff and not very pleasant and for a moment Theresa thought about cutting the call, but her desire to talk to someone about the awful suspicions she was having, was too great, so she stuttered, "I'd like to speak to someone dealing with the murder of Sally Smith."

After a few clicks, she heard, "DC Douglas."

"Um," Theresa had no idea who DC Douglas was, so she repeated, "I'd like to speak to someone dealing with the murder of Sally Smith."

"I'm part of that team, ma'am, how can I help?"

"I, um, I might have some information that could be important."

"Very well, could I firstly have your name?"

"Theresa Dennison."

"Okay, Mrs Dennison…"

DC Douglas waited, but Theresa was having trouble spitting out the foul words, which were sticking to the sides of her mouth like candy floss. Could she really do this? But then she thought of the dismissive way Tim had treated her that morning and the lies he'd told her.

"Mrs Dennison?" DC Douglas prompted.

"What? Oh, sorry, yes, I think my husband might have something to do with it." Theresa tried to slow her speech down, but she was having trouble stopping the torrent of words now she was actually saying them out loud. "The murder. You see he was visiting the area the night she was killed and this morning he's just lied to me about what's happening tonight at the university and, you'll never believe this, but he tried to strangle me once when we were having sex. So you see, he could have something to do with it. You do see don't you?" Theresa increased her grip on the mobile.

"Is there anything else?

"What do you mean anything else? Isn't that enough?"

"I mean evidence, madam."

"Evidence?" Theresa was stunned into silence for a moment. She hadn't thought about that. How stupid of her.

"Yes, evidence," he repeated.

"Well, no. No, I suppose not."

"So it's just a feeling then?"

"Well, when you put it that way."

"What's your husband's name and what does he do?"

"Tim… Professor Tim Dennison."

"Professor?"

"Yes, in criminology."

"Really?" the young man sounded doubtful, as if he was thinking this was nothing but a crack-pot call.

"Really," Theresa said with more determination that she actually felt. "So what are you going to do about it?"

"I'm not sure there's much we can do if all you have is a feeling. Perhaps if you think of anything else? Or if anything else happens? You could give us a call again then."

"You mean if anyone else is killed?" she spat.

"Not at all, Mrs Dennison, please calm down."

"Look, don't bother," she said feeling humiliated, which made her angrier. "I'll sort it out myself."

Theresa cut the call, threw the mobile onto the grass and then promptly burst into tears, feeling once more out manoeuvred by a man.

Ciaran

Ciaran Douglas looked at the telephone handset he'd just replaced and wondered about the woman who'd made the call. Should he draw it to Anderson's attention? Or would the guv feel he was becoming as loopy as the woman he'd just been speaking to? But what if Mrs Dennison was right and something else did happen and he'd done nothing about it? He chewed absently on his finger nail before coming to a decision. Pushing his chair away from his desk, he stood and poked his head around Anderson's door.

"Guv, can I have a word?"

"Mmm," Anderson said through a mouthful of something or other. Whatever it was it must have had contained the chocolate which was sprinkled all over the front of his shirt and tie.

"Um, with everyone?"

Once again Anderson nodded, so Ciaran rounded up Holly and Crane and once they were all lounging around the table and looking at him expectantly, he recounted the conversation he'd just had with Mrs Dennison.

"And?" asked Anderson

"And I don't know what to do, guv. So I thought it

best to bring it to the team."

"Oh, so we can collectively get it wrong," laughed Crane.

As Ciaran's face flamed Anderson said, "Ciaran, take no notice and, Crane, behave yourself."

"Sorry," Crane said. "But joking apart, there's not much we can do, is there?"

"I could dig into his background," offered Holly. "See if he's got any previous and who knows what I might find out online."

Ciaran could have kissed her for taking his dilemma seriously, but the thought of kissing Holly, once more, brought the flush of embarrassment to his face that he was having to deal with rather more often than he'd like.

"How likely is our choker to kill again?" asked Crane. "That's the nub of it from what I can see."

"I might be able to help with that too," said Holly, fishing a small tablet from one of the many voluminous pockets in her cargo pants. "May I, guv?"

"Please do, Holly."

After a few swipes she read, "According to scientific evidence when the brain is deprived of oxygen, it induces a lucid, semi-hallucinogenic state called hypoxia. Now, it's a condition in which the body as a whole, or a region of the body, is deprived of adequate oxygen supply. And when this is combined with orgasm, the rush is said to be no less powerful than cocaine, and this is the bit that is particularly telling; it's highly addictive."

"Oh," said Crane looking troubled.

Ciaran could feel a palpable tension. It was as if their collective fear was filling the room, pushing out all the air from it and making his head swim. He realised Holly was still speaking.

"Hallucinogenic states of mind brought about by

chronic hypoxia may be similar to the hallucinations experienced by climbers at altitude and could be a reason why mountain climbing is said to be very addictive."

"So our choker is addicted to this hypoxia?" asked Anderson.

"That's what I think," agreed Holly. "It seems the increased pleasure results in the body producing more endorphins as it approaches the state of asphyxia. Normal sex won't be enough for him anymore. He'll be craving the ultimate rush that only hypoxia can give him."

"What if that's not what he's becoming addicted to?"

"Sorry?" asked Anderson.

Crane continued, "What if the ultimate rush for him is killing the woman he's choking?"

Ciaran closed his eyes and wished very hard he could be somewhere, anywhere, other than at work trying to catch a sadistic murderer, who could very well be unable to stop killing again. But when he opened them, he was still there. As was their killer. Ciaran could feel his malevolent presence, as though he was in the room with them.

Watching them.

Mocking them.

Theresa

That night, Tim didn't get home until nearly midnight. Pretending to be asleep, Theresa lay as still as she could, eyes closed, listening to her husband undress, bang around in the bathroom and then slide into bed beside her. She could smell soap and toothpaste, but they couldn't completely disguise the smell of stale alcohol and cigarettes emanating from his skin and hair. Hoping against hope that he wouldn't turn and reach for her, she held her breath as he settled into his normal sleeping position, back towards her and covers pulled up to his neck.

She soon heard his breathing become deep and regular as he fell into a sound sleep. He twitched once or twice and then stilled. She was safe. He didn't want her tonight. She couldn't imagine ever wanting to make love to him again. Not whilst the torturous thoughts were wheeling around in her brain. But then she couldn't remember the last time they'd had sex. Not since the neck incident she didn't think. About six months ago. Had he gone off her because she wouldn't stoop to his perverted level? But then again they hadn't had sex much before that either. She didn't know whether it was awful they had so little sex. Maybe it was what all couples did - gradually slip out of the habit? Was that what was normal? Who was to say what was normal?

Sleep was further away than ever. Tim was oblivious to her twists and turns as she tried to get comfortable in the hope sleep would come. But the harder she chased it, the more awake she became. Glancing at the clock she saw it was 1.00am, so she decided to get up and make a hot drink. Perhaps some hot chocolate would do the trick. That and a boring book.

Once in the kitchen, she put the kettle on and grabbed a sachet out of the nearby cupboard. Turning to get a mug, she saw Tim's mobile phone on the kitchen table. That was strange. He normally didn't let it out of his sight and at night time it was always next to his bed. A treacherous thought began to worm its way into her head. She couldn't. She shouldn't. She mustn't. She tried to convince herself, but it wasn't working.

The kettle boiled unnoticed, as Theresa's focus was firmly on the mobile on the table. As if not part of her anymore, her hand reached out and picked it up. She knew Tim didn't have a password on his phone, so she pressed the switch on the side and the screen lit up. Breathing hard, she grabbed the nearest chair and sank into it, still holding the phone.

What if there was something incriminating on it? Those sexy text message things people sent these days; sexting or something. She'd heard people even sent photos of each other in provocative poses. Her hand shook and she nearly dropped the phone. Putting it back on the table, she started to make her hot chocolate, hoping the hot drink would calm her and warm her up. She had nothing on her feet and they were freezing, so she sat back down, hooking them around the chair legs and, with her hands cradling the mug, she sipped at the drink.

The light went off on Tim's phone, but it didn't help. She was still desperate to find out what it contained but terrified of what she might find. When had she become so indecisive? Since she'd been married, she realised. Tim was the one who did everything. He was the organiser. The household bills, the mortgage, the bank account - they were all in his name. He'd always told her it was her job to look after the children and his to look after everything else. She'd just accepted it as normal. But she wasn't so sure anymore. Was that normal as well? Or not?

She realised her drink was cooling, so she put it on the table and in a moment of clarity realised she was better off knowing what was going on, than not. All the amount of speculation in the world wouldn't make her feel better. Only the truth. And if it was bad? Then she'd just have to deal with it.

The phone felt heavy in her hand, as heavy as her heart, as she started up the phone and began with the text messages.

The following evening life returned to its regular rhythm and full of beef casserole and red wine, Theresa was feeling better, slightly tipsy if anything, but at least that was healthier than the constant state of anxiety she'd been in. She stole a glance at Tim, who was seemingly involved in a new drama on the television. Last night when she'd looked at his phone she hadn't found anything incriminating. No sexy texts or photos. No liaisons. No voicemails from another woman.

Alright, so there hadn't been anything on the phone.

Nothing. No logs of missed, received or dialled numbers. No texts received or sent. Whilst that pleased her at the time, as she'd found nothing incriminating, she'd also begun to realise it was slightly strange behaviour to clear everything off the mobile. On her phone she had stored messages from her sons, Tim and even the optician and dentist reminding her she was due for check-ups. She often meant to delete them but never seemed to get around to it. Did it mean that Tim had cleared the history on purpose? But why would he have done such a thing?

She picked up her phone and turned it on to check for any messages. It was a temperamental old thing and sometimes she didn't get an alert for messages or emails. But there was nothing new. No one urgently trying to get hold of her. No one inviting her to a coffee morning. No one asking her to volunteer for this, that or the other.

As the television programme drew to a close, she could feel Tim watching her. "What are you doing?" he asked.

"Just checking for new messages and stuff."

"Anything?"

"No, nothing urgent," she lied, not wanting him to know how empty her life was at the moment. "Actually, it's a bit clogged up," she said, "but I'm not sure how to delete stuff. Can you help me?"

"Sorry, love, don't know myself. I had a problem with mine a couple of days ago it wasn't ringing when someone called me. Being a complete idiot when it comes to mobile phones, someone in the department sorted it out."

"What did they do?"

"They had to reset the thing. I've lost all my contacts, texts and photos, but at least it saved the cost of a new phone. Anyway," he said standing, "are you coming up?"

"Yes, I'll be there in a bit. I'll just tidy the kitchen first."

Theresa watched him leave the room as her tears blurred the view of his back. The relief was enormous, so much so she could have sat there and sobbed. But he'd hear her, so she sniffed, wiped at her eyes with her hand and took her phone and her now empty glass through to the kitchen.

Such a simple explanation, after so many hours of worry. She felt a bit of a fool to say the least. In her suspicion she'd never thought of his phone breaking. So there was nothing sinister going on after all. It was all in her head.

Going back into the lounge, she collected Tim's glass and his mobile, putting it next to hers on the kitchen table. He'd obviously forgotten to take it up with him again, so she would do it for him.

After hand-washing the wine glasses, she began to wipe them dry, when she heard a noise. She was sure it was a bell or something similar. A phone ringing? Looking at the two mobiles on the kitchen table, neither of them were lit, ringing, or buzzing. How strange. She was sure she'd heard a phone. She could have got confused with the ringing of the glass as she'd dried it, she supposed.

Putting the glass and tea-towel down she moved into the hall. There it was again. An insistent ring - which abruptly stopped as she reached the bottom of the stairs. Straining to hear, she heard the low rumble of Tim's voice. She couldn't make out any words, but he was definitely having a conversation.

Running back into the kitchen she finished drying the glasses and put them away. Grabbing the mobiles she then turned off the lights downstairs and walked up to the bedroom, the sense of dread heightening with every step she took. She felt like she was in an old fashioned sea faring movie and was being punished by having to walk the plank. She teetered on the edge, feeling the world tip beneath her feet. With a deep breath she pushed open the door to find Tim in bed, on his side, covers pulled up to his neck.

"Tim," she called.

"Yes?"

"Did I just hear a mobile phone ring up here?"

"No," his head popped up from the pillow. "In fact my mobile's not here."

"I know," Theresa said. "You left it in the kitchen."

"Then you must be mistaken," he said as he did his impression of a turtle, retreating into his shell of covers.

"I must be going a bit gaga then."

"Okay." Tim snuggled further under the covers and within minutes was snoring.

But Theresa didn't sleep. Couldn't sleep. She could have sworn she'd heard a mobile ringing and then Tim answering it. She needed to find it, but suspected it was well hidden. She would have her chance tomorrow night when Tim was away, speaking at Portsmouth University as part of their debating programme. Mind you, she realised as she turned over to try and get comfortable, if he does have a secret mobile, he'll probably have it with him. Resigned to the fact she might never find it, she fell into a light, troubled sleep, dreaming dreams that featured mobile phones and planks of wood.

Boy

So now I know the real story of Sleeping Beauty. She was called Talia and a Prince found her asleep in her chamber in the castle. Stunned by her beauty he climbed into bed with her. Well, who wouldn't? It was as if she were handed to him on a plate. I wish I could find someone like that. Someone who would let me do anything to them. Someone who wouldn't scream, or wriggle, or hit me and tell me to go away.

That's what's been happening at school. When I find a girl I like, she's invariably horrible to me. I tied one up once, and she made such fuss I had to let her go. I kept telling her it felt nice to be tied up, but she didn't agree.

Daddy was called into the Headmaster, because she'd told on me. He was very angry. He tied me to the bed as I'm too big for the cupboard under the stairs now. He stretched my arms up above my head and tied my wrists to the ends of the bed head. Then he spread my legs and tied my ankles to the bed. Did I say I was naked? Daddy had made me take off all of my clothes first.

I don't know how long he left me there, but even though I was relieved when he came back to set me free, as my arms were hurting and my hands going numb, in a strange way I wanted him to do it again. Sometimes at night I hold my arms out, pretending they are tied to the bed. I spread my legs and pretend they are tied to the bed as well. It makes me very excited, if you know what I mean. Afterwards I feel so relieved and relaxed and fall into a deep sleep.

Talia Sun and Moon.

Holly

Holly sighed with frustration. So far Sally's mobile had revealed nothing out of the ordinary. No texts arranging a meeting, no calls from unknown numbers. Whilst she hadn't really expected a lead to land in her lap easily, it would have been nice for once. She chewed the end of a pen, deep in thought.

So, the next move was onto the apps. These would be where she would get an indication of what sort of woman Sally had been; who she chatted to and what the messages revealed. Was she lonely? Bored? Broke?

Diving in, she decided to tackle the emails first, but after a while it became clear there was nothing much there. Most of the emails referred to work. Sally had been an accounts clerk at an events company. Whilst that may have seemed like a really interesting job, Sally was at the blunt end of the company. Sorting out payments and chasing up unpaid invoices was the extent of her involvement. Others were at the sharp end, attending many corporate events for clients as diverse as financial services and pharmaceuticals, to record labels and publishers. There was the occasional company-wide 'thank you' consisting of gift vouchers and tickets to football matches, but it was a far cry from the glamorous city job Sally pretended it was to her friends.

Her Facebook page was rather more illuminating. She promoted events her company was involved in and, in the private messages, Holly read of Sally's disappointment that she was not attending them herself. Various excuses were used; 'I'm needed in the office', 'super-busy at the moment' and 'I'm sure it will be my turn next!' But it never seemed to be her turn. WhatsApp produced similar conversation threads.

A background check and genealogy tree had revealed Sally was an only child whose parents were both dead. She had an aunt, Jean Burton and a cousin, Jean's daughter Amanda, but she didn't seem to have had much contact with them, apart from at Christmas.

But, of course, they'd just had to endure the worst kind of contact. The local police in Middlesbrough where they lived had been to inform them of her death. Amanda had made the long journey from the North East of England with her mother, who was required to make the formal identification. Ciaran had been with them at the mortuary and, by the look on his face when he'd come back, the two women had been devastated. He'd confessed to Holly the identification of a body by the family was worse than enduring an autopsy. During those he managed to stay relatively removed from the fact that the victim had been alive once, but standing there with Jean and Amanda, as they'd stared down at Sally's dead body, had made it far more real. The anguish of her family members had made him wonder what it would be like if it was his sister, or mum even, lying there? How would he feel? Bloody awful, Holly had thought as she'd looked into his dull eyes. She'd sent him out to buy her a green tea, just so she wouldn't have to look at his face that reminded her of a Halloween mask, all dark shadows under his cheek bones and grimacing mouth.

"Anything?" Crane asked as he passed her desk.

"What?" Holly shook herself away from her depressing thoughts.

"On Sally?"

"Oh, sorry, guv, um, well it's all a bit pathetic really."

"What is?" Crane rolled over a chair and sat down, his face contorting with pain as usual, from his injury.

"Sally's life. It's all normal and humdrum, but lacking in something, somehow."

"Explain."

So Holly told Crane what she'd found out so far.

"Okay," Crane said. "So, she was lonely, unfulfilled at work and living with a girl who was away most of the time."

"Exactly," said Holly, pleased that Crane agreed with her assessment.

"Boyfriend?"

"No sign of one anywhere."

"Bugger." Crane scratched at his beard, something Holly had seen him do many times before when he was thinking. He scratched the scar just visible under the short dark stubble he called a beard.

"Its difficult work without her laptop, guv."

Holly for some reason felt the need to defend her work. It was probably because Crane was so bloody good at his job. His analytical mind seemed wired in pretty much the same way as her own and, as a result, Holly found him easier to work with than other members of the team. Being an ex-soldier he was brief, to the point, and was always first completing a task. The only downside being he tended to give someone a job to do, but then did it himself, completing it before the poor unsuspecting member of the team had even started.

"If I were you, I'd investigate what we don't know and see where that leads."

"Sorry, guv?"

"Did she have any other social media accounts? Was she a member of any dating sites? What was her internet browsing history? She must have made contact with her killer somehow."

Holly grinned. "On it, guv," she said, but she was talking to his back as Crane was already on his way over to his desk. He was limping heavily and sank into his chair as though it were a life raft, immediately opening his drawer, grabbing a pill bottle and shaking several into his hand. He dry swallowed them, before quickly returning the container to his desk. She wondered what the tablets were and how many he should actually be taking. She suspected one or two at a time, not a handful.

She turned back to her computer, but when she stole a glance at Crane a few minutes later, he'd visibly relaxed and was leaning back in his chair reading a file.

Crane

Crane sat in the passenger seat, watching the countryside roll by, as Anderson drove them along the A3, heading for Portsmouth. On his lap was a file Ciaran had pulled together for them from information supplied by the local police. Most of the drive was through the South Downs National Park and it was a far preferable view to the photographs contained in the file.

"Earth to Crane," piped up Anderson.

"What? Oh, sorry," Crane pulled his eyes away from the green vista and looked at Anderson.

"Come on, you're supposed to be reading the file to me."

Crane sighed not wanting to do any such thing, but flipped open the cover. "Okay, the murder victim is Charlie Keating, 24 and he was a customer service representative for a mobile phone company. He lived in a flat on his own, above a row of mostly empty shops, near to the town centre."

"So, on the face of it, his death is unrelated to Sally's murder, as she was female and this is the murder of a young male."

Crane nodded, then stopped as he realised Anderson

couldn't see him. So he said, "Exactly, but it's the circumstances of his death makes it of interest to us. His hands were bound with scarves to the bed and a third was found around his neck."

"So far so good."

"The investigating officers saw similar sized bruising from thumbs on his neck, to those on Sally, located over the carotid artery and there was evidence of sexual lubricant and condoms."

"Is the body still in the flat?"

"No, it's been transferred to the local mortuary, but Major Martin has been called in to do the autopsy as this death could be related to ours."

"Excellent. Now put that away and help me navigate our way around Portsmouth."

It took the best part of half an hour to find the flat and then a parking space, but eventually the car stopped and Crane climbed out with the help of his stick. The only problem with car journeys was his knee became locked and his hip went to sleep. He rolled drunkenly in Anderson's wake, gradually getting the feeling back in his leg. He groaned when he saw the metal stairs outside the back of the parade of shops, but grabbed the handrail and between his hand and his stick, managed to get to the top. Anderson spoke to the uniformed policeman guarding a blue painted front door and then they were in.

The small space contained just three rooms: kitchen/lounge, bathroom and bedroom. The pungent smell of weed had pervaded the soft furnishings, making Crane cough. He had no time for drugs. Drug users were quickly identified in the Army through random drug tests and users were given their marching orders. Alcohol was the preferred drug of choice for most soldiers. However, all that was no concern of his anymore and with a struggle he turned his mind away from his beloved army, back to the present and the civilian police investigation.

They began in the bedroom, comparing the room now with the photographs in the file. The bed dominated the space, there being little room for anything else other than one bedside table. The other side of the bed was pushed up against the wall in an effort to make the space seem larger than it actually was.

"No bed linen," Crane said.

"No, it was found clean in the washing machine."

"Ah," said Crane looking at the photo of Charlie's body, naked and spread eagled on the bed. The flash had easily picked out the marks on his neck. His skin looked grey in the black and white photograph.

"How long had he been dead? Do we have a timeframe for his murder?"

"Not yet, but Charlie was at work yesterday, so it must have happened overnight at some point."

Having seen enough, Crane limped into the largest room in the apartment. Two threadbare settees were over by the window, placed facing a large television. Under the window was an old computer desk, one that had a pull-out tray for a keyboard. Crane pulled it out but there was nothing there, just four marks where laptop legs or keyboard legs had been. He flicked through the file. No laptop, computer or mobile phones were found in the flat. Yet another similarity between this murder and Sally's.

Crane turned as Anderson entered the room, but his leg failed to obey the instructions from his brain and as he twisted he fell to the floor.

"Shit! This fucking leg!"

"Not to worry, Crane, up you get," and Anderson

held out a helping hand.

"Jesus, it fucking kills. And stop being so bloody nice about it," Crane grumbled.

"For God's sake, calm down and get up. Here."

But Crane didn't take Anderson's hand. He'd twisted as he'd fallen, so his head was now underneath the computer desk.

"Crane? Stop pissing about and get up, will you?"

"Hang on, Derek, there's something stuck to the bottom of the tray here."

"You sure?"

"Of course I'm bloody sure!"

"Alright, alright, hang on," and Anderson joined Crane on the floor. "Well I'll be buggered, so there is. Come on, get up and we'll tip the table over."

Crane managed to struggle upright and watched as Anderson up-ended the rickety desk. Pulling out his mobile phone he took several pictures and then took an evidence bag and latex gloves out of his pocket.

"What is it?" Crane asked as he hadn't been close enough to read what was on the piece of paper stuck to the underside of the keyboard tray.

"Looks to me like his list of emails and social media accounts, together with their user names and passwords," said Anderson as he pulled on the gloves.

"Well, what do you know," Crane grinned. "We've found something for Holly to work with at last."

Theresa

There was only a small piece on the local news that evening. They said a young man had been found murdered in his flat in Portsmouth. There were no other details available but a post mortem was taking place and a team from the Hampshire Major Crimes Unit had been called in.

Major Crimes.

The people who were investigating the murder of Sally.

Theresa berated herself for having an over active imagination. For seeing connections that just weren't there. Sally's murder was in Aldershot and the latest was in Portsmouth. And there was no indication from the news broadcast they were connected.

But Tim hadn't come home last night. He'd sent a text saying it would be the early hours before he got back from Portsmouth, so he'd just go to his room at the university and stay there. He had a sofa bed for the times when he'd be late and didn't want to disturb her sleep. He'd said it wasn't fair and he'd never be so disrespectful of her.

She couldn't see it herself. Thought of it as something

else that kept them apart. They were more and more leading separate lives. Well, he was. She didn't have much of a life to lead if she was honest. Every time she'd suggested something to fill her time, such as getting a job, he'd said that she really didn't need to. They didn't need the money, so why bother? 'Enjoy your free time,' he'd said. 'You spent all those years looking after the boys and this is your reward.'

But it didn't feel like much of a reward.

On the night of Sally's murder, he'd been staying in a hotel in the Aldershot area.

On the night of Charlie's murder he'd been in Portsmouth.

Her head felt as though it would spin right off her neck. Her body was a punch bag as her thoughts swung backwards and forwards and she felt every one as though it were a blow to her stomach.

He could be guilty. He could be no such thing.

He was in the two towns on the nights of both murders. A pure co-incidence nothing more.

He had a penchant for 'that' sort of sex. Don't be silly he only tried it once.

He had a secret mobile phone. You could have been hearing things.

Stumbling into the kitchen, she grabbed a shot glass from a cupboard in the corner. Hanging onto the freezer she took out a bottle of vodka one of the boys had given them for Christmas and insisted it had to stay cold. She'd done as he suggested, but had no idea why. Until she filled the glass and downed the vodka in one. The shock of the ice cold liquid going down her throat, soon gave way to the fire spreading through her belly from the strong alcohol. She smiled. That was better. Perhaps she could sneak in another one. Before she could change her mind, she the refilled the glass and drank it back. She staggered slightly, bumping against the freezer. She very definitely had had enough. Tim would be home soon. She'd have to appear normal.

But her hands couldn't help fluttering to her neck.

The following morning, the ringing of the phone interrupted Theresa's seemingly constant cleaning of the house. It was the only thing she had to do, the only thing she was allowed to do, and so was determined to do it well. She wiped the sweat off her brow with her hand and pushed away a few locks of hair that had escaped from the hair band tying it back into a ponytail.

"Hello?"

"Oh hi, Sally. It's Rose. I've got a date for your diary."

"What's it for?" Theresa was used to various functions at the university she was expected to attend alongside Tim, although there hadn't been any lately.

"Charity fund raiser. The Dean's pet charity needs an injection of cash, so he's hosting a dinner and charity auction."

"Fine. When is it?"

Theresa took down the details, scribbling away on the pad by the phone and said she'd put it in her diary. Rose hoped she was free on that night as it did mean so much to the Dean. Theresa said she understood its importance and assured Rose she would be there on Tim's arm, not mentioning her diary was empty and, in fact, unused. The pages as white and crisp and clean as they had been at the beginning of the year when she'd bought it, more in hope than necessity.

"Oh, I am glad," said Rose, "especially as you've had to miss the last few."

"Miss?" Time seemed to stand still as Theresa realised the implications of Rose's words. Missed. She'd never missed any function. At least none that she'd known of.

"Yes." But Rose was hesitant. "You've been ill… I hope you're feeling better now?"

"Ill?" was all Theresa could manage. What had Tim being doing? Why hadn't she known about the invitations?

Trying hard to recover her composure, she said, "That'll be another late night for Tim, then," not wanting the conversation to linger on her supposed illness.

"Another?" It seemed it was Rose's turn to be taken aback.

"Yes, it was the early hours before he got back from Portsmouth. You know, he was a speaker at the debating society this week."

"Oh, right, I, um, yes of course, I must have forgotten about that one. Anyway, must dash, Glad you're feeling more yourself. Bye."

Theresa was left holding a dead telephone and pondering Rose's strange comments. It seemed Theresa had known nothing of her own mysterious illness and Rose had known nothing about a trip to Portsmouth. That was very strange as Rose never made a mistake. Theresa chewed her lip, thinking.

In the kitchen her laptop was open, so she went to it and in the search engine typed, Portsmouth University. Once on their website she clicked on the link for the debating society, pulling up their list of events.

There had been no debate last night. Actually there had been no debates for the past two months, due to the organiser falling ill. Normal service was hoped to be resumed next term.

She slammed the lid of her laptop closed. Why had

Tim been in Portsmouth? Had he even been in Portsmouth at all? He'd definitely been somewhere as he hadn't been at home. Breathing became difficult and her eyes were blinking uncontrollably. She grabbed a cloth and some cleaning fluid and began scrubbing the already sparkling hob.

Aldershot Mail Online

Has The Choker struck again?

The Aldershot News continues to bring you the latest stories that affect our local community and the wider Hampshire area. We understand the murder of a young man aged just 24 and living in Portsmouth, who has yet to be formally identified, has died in similar circumstances to our local girl Sally Sawyer.

Once again silk scarves have been mentioned and bruising was clearly visible on the poor man's neck. It seems that young men and women from the BDSM community are no longer safe and should take every precaution before meeting strangers for sex.

If this is linked to auto erotic asphyxiation, as the police assume, we must warn our readers that this is an extremely dangerous practice. Cutting off oxygen to the brain can lead to brain damage or even death. It is highly recommended this sexual practise be avoided at all costs.

Ciaran

Once he'd finished reading the online article, Ciaran handed the tablet back to Donna.

"So, now do you see why I called you?" she asked. "Is it true? Is this another victim, the same as Sally?"

"At the moment, we just don't know, Donna."

"But it could be?"

Ciaran was intrinsically an honest person, so he answered truthfully, "Yes, it could be."

"Oh my God." Donna fell into the hard chair by the desk in yet another anonymous hotel room. "Are you any nearer to catching him?"

"We're following up a few leads… that's all I can say at the moment."

Donna was looking alarmingly pale and she was swaying, her body threatening to fall off the chair, so he said, "Quick, put your head between your knees," and he lightly pushed her head downwards.

Once she had obeyed his instruction, he said, "I'll get you some water," and he ran to the small en-suite and grabbed a plastic cup, filling it with water from the tap.

"Here," he said returning, "try and sip some of this."

"Thanks," Donna mumbled and she sipped at the cup

Ciaran was holding for her. His ministrations had done the trick and slowly Donna's colour returned.

"So sorry," she said.

Ciaran crouched down before her and put the cup down. "It's okay."

"I'm just so frightened. What if he comes after me? I'm not sure I can move back into the flat. He knows where I live. He could think I can help you catch him!"

"Please, Donna, I'm sure that's not the case." Ciaran grabbed her hands in his and tried hard to ignore the frisson it caused. It was as though he'd had a small electric shock. "And anyway I'll always be available if you become frightened. Don't let this take over your life. That way he'll win, won't he, whoever he is?"

"Yes, yes, I suppose you're right," Donna took a couple of deep breaths. "So, it would be alright for me to call you? You know, if anything happens?"

"Definitely," agreed Ciaran, anxious to be Donna's knight in shining armour, pushing aside his doubts about whether it was entirely proper for him to like a woman connected to his murder investigation. He was still holding her hands in his and was amazed she hadn't pulled them away.

"Thanks, that makes me feel much better." Donna lifted her head and smiled at him, her frightened eyes making a mockery of the polished, professional persona she projected.

It was those eyes that did it and Ciaran found himself saying, "Look, I don't know about you but I need a drink. Shall we go downstairs to the bar?"

He was thrilled when Donna agreed with his impromptu suggestion.

Theresa

"Rose called today," Theresa said as she and Tim cleared the table after dinner. "About the charity thing for the Dean?"

"Oh, yes, I've brought home the official invitation. It's in my briefcase. Go and get it if you like."

"Alright," said Theresa walking into the hall, where Tim's briefcase rested on the floor by the front door.

She hadn't been able to resist mentioning it, half wondering if the function did exist, but then berating herself for over-reacting. Of course it was genuine and of course she would be going with Tim. It was just that she'd wondered if he would make an excuse for her absence and leave her at home, manipulating her once again and ensuring he had a night out on his own.

Laying the rather battered case flat on the floor, which Tim had had since his first post at the university, she clicked the clasps and raised the lid. There, on top of a couple of books, was a white envelope with, 'Professor and Mrs Dennison' written on it. Theresa reached for it, but then her hand stopped half way there, as she spied a flash of colour peeking out from under the books.

Rocking back on her heels, she stilled. Then, heart

racing and hands shaking, she plucked at it, feeling the silk slide under her fingers. The garish colours were bright against her white hands and the material whispered as she pulled it from one hand to the other. A little voice inside her whispered...

A colourful silk scarf found wound around her neck.

Hands tied to the bed.

Evidence of oxygen deprivation by choking.

She couldn't move. Her feet were stuck to the floor. She was unable to wrench her gaze from the scarf.

"Theresa!"

The sound of Tim's call made her jump and the scarf fell from her hands, breaking the spell. She grabbed the scarf and the invitation and walked through to the kitchen, leaving the briefcase where it was.

It took all her willpower to keep her voice even. "What's this?" She held up the scarf.

"Oh, it belongs to Rose. She left it in the car when I gave her a lift home."

"Why is it in your briefcase?"

"To remind me to give it to her. You know what I'm like," he laughed. "My memory is rubbish and I'd leave it in the car for a week. Pop it back in the case would you?"

Theresa nodded and walked back into the hall in a daze. Tim said it belonged to Rose. A perfectly plausible excuse for having a woman's scarf in his briefcase. But did she believe him? As she let go of the scarf it slithered into the case, reminding Theresa of a snake. A poisonous snake, worming its way into their marriage.

Boy

We're studying crime and the punishment of criminals at school, a subject I seem to be doing rather well at, as I find it so interesting. We're on our way to the Clink Prison Museum, built on the site of the first ever prison. That fluttering feeling is back and I'm revelling in it. Stupid John, who has been allocated as my partner, keeps wittering on about home, his brothers and the model plane he is building. I keep my mouth shut and ignore him most of the time, staring out of the coach window as we crawl along in the London traffic.

With a hiss of brakes and a cheer from the class, we arrive. Everyone makes their straggling way to the door of the museum. I push to the front, with John trailing behind me, as I'm determined not to miss a minute, or a word, or the opportunity to handle the instruments of torture.

A man appears and tells us we'll be learning how inmates were treated and the conditions they lived in. We will have the opportunity to handle original historical artefacts relating to crime and punishment, used both in the Clink Prison and nationally. My hands itch at his words and if I'm not careful someone will see how eager

I am to get started.

At the sight of the manacles I nearly swoon like a heroine in one of my favourite gothic novels. They are much heavier than I thought they would be and as I hold the weight of them in my hands my imagination runs riot. The satisfying clink of the chains, the chill of the iron, the huge plates fashioned to fit around wrists, all contribute to my determination to get a pair of my own. I wonder what it would feel like to be manacled and then hung from the ceiling.

Left there, waiting for my tormentor. Not knowing when he, or she, would return.

I walk straight past the wax skeletal prisoners, but when we get to the large wooden chair, well things start to look up. Being the first in line, John and I are allowed to sit in it and demonstrate to the rest of the class. The old oak wooden structure is bigger than we are, but I am still able to pin John's head against the back of it, immobilising him with the large leather straps around his forehead. There are similar straps for his wrists, securing them on the arms of the chair and his dangling legs are bound in leather also. Standing up I look at him closely. His face is pale with small beads of sweat dotted over his forehead. His hands are clenched and his eyes large. Moving behind him, I grab the wheel that will raise the back of the chair, lifting him out of the seat and stretching and pulling his body.

His screams alert the guide and the teacher, who both shriek at me to stop. The guide rushes to John and releases the leather straps and the teacher grabs my arm, pulling me away from the instrument of torture.

"What the hell do you think you are doing, boy?"

"Having a bit of fun," I reply.

His face goes a putrid, puce colour. "The Headmaster

will hear about this," he hisses at me and pushes me towards the back of the snake of students. But I can't suppress my grin, nor hide my excitement.

The Clink - the prison that gave its name to all others.

Crane

Whilst Holly was working on the online investigation into Charlie Keating's murder, Crane and Anderson were stumped. Once again the body and the flat had been cleaned down with bleach. There was no phone or laptop in the property. So the only option left was CCTV. Portsmouth police had given them access to recorded footage from the local cameras for the night of Charlie's murder.

After what seemed like hours of fruitless viewing, Crane needed a break and a fag. Doing his best to stop smoking, Crane was trying electronic cigarettes but ended up using both; smoking cigarettes during the day and his e-cigarette at home. He would have used the electronic version at work, but for some reason they weren't allowed in the office either. He had no idea why. If he was blowing out harmless water vapour, why couldn't he use it in the office? He put it down to another case of health and safety gone mad. So he clumped his way out of the office, into the car park, where he leaned against the wall and lit up.

As he smoked he mulled over the two cases. Something he did consciously and unconsciously during an investigation. Tina, his wife, was used to him being remote at times, as he'd been an investigator for all of their married life. She sometimes grumbled about being like a one parent family as he was away from home such a lot, and even when he was at home he was obsessed with some case or other and walked around the house in a daze. But she always confessed she wouldn't have it any other way. Part of Crane was better than none, she'd told him. Crane had had no answer to that, finding sentiment hard to deal with. He was so used to containing his feelings, holding back his emotions and dealing only in facts, he found it hard to open up in his personal life.

But his focus, for now, had to be the two murders, not Tina and their young son Daniel, despite how awful it sounded. They were chasing a bi-sexual murderer, addicted to the euphoric rush that breath control play brought. But Crane was very much afraid he, or she, was addicted to killing as well. Crane was convinced their murderer was a man, but Holly wasn't so sure, being more inclined towards the feminist point of view that it could just as easily be a woman. She was convinced that with a victim already disarmed by the confused state the sexual practise brought, it would be fairly easy for a murderer to go one step further.

But all of that was conjecture for now. They needed solid evidence, which was proving elusive.

A sudden stab in his hip caused his leg to buckle underneath him and he clawed at the wall to try and keep upright. He ended up leaning against it, half upright, like a drunken solider at the end of a night out in Aldershot. The pain left him gasping and he fumbled in his pocket for a Tramadol. To be honest he wasn't sure how many he was supposed to take in a day. He thought it was three. One in the morning and two at night. But somewhere someone had said he could have an emergency one, if the pain got particularly bad. The trouble was he frequently lost count and just went with having one when the pain was bad. Which, to be honest, was most of the day.

Sliding down the wall and sitting on the cold floor, he swallowed a tablet and stayed where he was for a while until the debilitating pain subsided. Crane was just considering a second cigarette, when his phone whistled the electronic version of woody woodpecker. Dragging it out of his pocket it was a WhatsApp from Holly. *Got something, guv.* So putting the second cigarette on hold for now, he hauled himself up and turned and fought his way through the obstacles of stairs and doors, back to the office.

He'd only just poked his head around the door to the main CID floor when Holly rushed over.

"Got something, guv!"

"I know, I know, I'm here now."

"Crane!" Anderson shouted from his office door. "Get in here, I've got something!"

"Um," Crane dithered as Holly jigged up and down beside him. "Look, Holly, come with me so you can tell whatever it is to Anderson at the same time. Sorry, but DI Anderson outranks you and me, come to that."

Holly grinned and followed his slow progress across the floor.

"Ciaran, you best come too," said Crane as they reached his desk. "I'm sure you don't want to miss the party."

And so the three of them arrived at Anderson's office door much to the DI's surprise. "Oh," he said as they took seats around the table, which was covered in files and photographs and reports.

"Holly here has something for us," Crane explained. "So I thought we could hear your news and hers."

"I might as well go first as I'm the boss," Anderson tried to look important by puffing his chest out and failed miserably as they all fell about laughing, as his stomach outranked his chest. "Bugger off you lot," he grumbled, but as he then grinned good-naturedly, Crane thought that at last they must have something to work with, hence Anderson's good mood.

"Crane and I have been working through the CCTV sent from Portsmouth," began Anderson. "And while Crane here was skiving outside, filling his lungs with contaminates, I saw a Suzuki Jeep in the area from a private CCTV camera that just shows the opening to a multi-story car park a few minutes' walk to the flats above the shops where Charlie lived. The Jeep arrived about 8pm and then left at 2.30 am. But I can't get a good enough image to get the licence plate."

"Do you want me to see if I can enhance it?"

"Thanks, Holly that would be great."

"Will do, guv."

"Doesn't the car park have the licence plate?" asked Ciaran. "Many of them read your number plate when you enter and leave."

"I wish, but no such luck," said Anderson. "I asked the local police that. But it's an old one that's been there many years and as the area is subject to redevelopment in the future, the owners hadn't seen any point in investing in new technology. So, your turn, Holly, what do you have for us?"

"I've been checking out Charlie's on-line presence to see if there is any correlation between the two victims, and trying to find anyone they were both friends with, who could be the killer. But I've not come up with anything so far. However, he does have a dating site account, so I've put a request into the administrators to see if they have an account under Sally's email address as well."

Crane felt a shiver of excitement. Two leads to work with. Maybe they were getting somewhere at last.

Theresa

Theresa had started her round of cleaning the house early, so by mid-day she was finished and all she had to look forward to for the rest of the day was starting all over again. She pulled off her rubber gloves and as she did so she caught sight of her bleach splattered jeans. Buying a new pair seemed a fairly good reason for going out, so she ran upstairs to change. Once ready, she checked the upstairs bathroom and the en-suite, just to make sure she hadn't missed any marks, or, heaven forbid, left any stains on the toilet. Happy that they were clean, at least for the moment, she went downstairs to check the kitchen was sparkling. After running her finger over the work surfaces and closely inspecting the sink, she was happy that the house was clean enough to leave.

Pausing to collect her car keys from the hall table, she just had to check the downstairs cloakroom. Confident the small space smelled of disinfectant and that there wasn't a mark to be seen, she opened the front door and went out to her car. Her little Suzuki Jimny Jeep sat on the driveway and she carefully backed it out onto the road and was away.

As she drove, she became aware of something rolling

around the inside of the car, on the floor. Pulling over, she found the culprit. An empty plastic bottle of water. Tim must have left it when he last used the car. He really must learn to take better care of her Jeep and she'd make sure to mention it tonight. What was the point of her working hard to keep the interior spotless, if he messed the car up every time he used it?

Arriving at the Oracle Shopping Centre in Reading town centre, Theresa parked the car on a fairly empty floor, so she was less likely to get dints in the side from people opening their car doors. She walked towards the shopping centre past the many food outlets and her stomach rumbled at the delicious smells wafting around her. She didn't want too much to eat, didn't fancy a burger or chicken, so settled on a Subway and coffee. As she walked along, turning over in her mind the various fillings they had to choose from, she passed an Italian restaurant. Glancing through the window, wondering if she should have a pizza instead, she stopped to check the menu pasted to the glass.

But she suddenly went off the idea when she saw a familiar back, sitting at a table towards the far end of the eatery. She was sure it was Tim's jacket. Let's face it, how many other men wore tweed jackets with elbow patches on? As she watched, he threw back his head with laughter and raised his glass. He chinked it with his companion and took a drink of what looked like red wine.

Theresa turned and leaned her back against the pane of glass, head swimming, unable to think clearly. Telling herself to remain calm and breathe, she fumbled for her mobile phone. Turning sideways, she peered around the menu board. Yes, he was still there. She scrolled through her contacts list, pressing the button to connect her with Tim. Watching him closely she saw him grab his phone from his pocket and answer it.

"Hi, love," he said. "Everything alright?"

"Yes, fine," Theresa said. "I was just wondering if you'd pick up a bottle of wine on your way home tonight. I'm a bit bogged down with the cleaning and can't be bothered to go out."

"Sure," he said.

"What you up to? Busy?"

"Yes, I'm afraid so. Just having a sandwich at my desk. No rest for the wicked eh? See you at home," and he finished the call.

Theresa saw him replace his phone and grab his wine glass once again, leaning over the table to talk to his mysterious friend.

Feeling sick, Theresa stumbled away from the restaurant back towards the canal, where she sank onto a bench.

'No peace for the wicked,' he'd said. Well he'd got that right, she decided. It was time to find out what Tim was really up to. And time she phoned the police again, this time to tell them about the Portsmouth trip. All thoughts of buying new jeans forgotten, she was planning what to do about catching her lying, cheating, murdering husband, as she pulled her mobile phone from her fake Gucci handbag.

Ciaran

"For God's sake," Holly shouted and banged down the telephone receiver.

"Whoa girl, what the matter?" Ciaran was rather alarmed to see his normally placid co-worker so angry. Her eyes were blazing and she banged her computer keyboard down for good measure.

"Bloody dating sites, that's what the matter!" Holly was still shouting and attracting the attention of the other policemen and women in the large open plan office.

"How about a coffee to calm you down?"

Ciaran deduced from Holly's piercing stare that yet again he'd said the wrong thing.

"Oh, right, no caffeine, sorry." To be honest if this was Holly without caffeine, he'd hate to see her with it. "Come on spit it out, what's the matter?"

"The dating people won't tell me if Sally and Charlie were members of their sites. 'Not without a warrant', they're all saying. Jesus, it's a murder investigation. What's wrong with these people? Who is it going to hurt if they just tell me?"

"I guess they feel they have a reputation to keep," said Ciaran, "No one would trust them with their personal data otherwise."

That got him another withering look.

"I haven't got time for this bullshit," Holly spat, but Ciaran detected a slight slump of resignation in her shoulders.

"I tell you what, give me their details and I'll draw up the warrants. What about that?"

"And what am I supposed to do in the meantime?"

"What about where the two victims grew up?"

"Nothing."

"Where they went to school?"

"Nothing."

Ciaran was praying for a miracle as he was getting nowhere. Then he had a light bulb moment. "Where they worked? Anything there?"

She glared at him. Ciaran didn't know if it was a good sign or a bad sign and held his breath.

"You bloody star," she said. "They could have used their work computers to help remain anonymous. Forget about those sites for the moment," she demanded. "Help me get access to their work computers. Use some of your boyish charm, so we don't have to wait for warrants for those as well."

Ciaran pulled up the details on his screen and reached for the phone on his desk. Before he could lift the receive it rang. "Sorry, Holly," he said. "I'd better answer this," secretly hoping it might be Donna. But it wasn't. It was from the woman he hoped never to hear from again.

"DC Douglas? Its Mrs Dennison, Theresa Dennison. I don't know if you remember me?"

"Oh yes, Mrs Dennison, I do." Ciaran closed his eyes. Then, aware that he wasn't being very polite, said, "What can I do for you?"

"That murder in Portsmouth, are you on the case?"

"We certainly have an interest in it, yes."

"That's what I thought!" The triumph in her voice rang clearly down the line. "I've got some information for you."

"Yes?"

"He was there that night. Or at least he said he was there. But he was lying. The event he was supposed to be attending didn't exist. It's all very fishy. So I thought I'd better tell you about it."

Ciaran very much wished she hadn't bothered. She was gibbering away and not making very much sense and he ended up taking the receiver away from his ear so Holly could hear Mrs Dennison squawking like a demented parrot. Holly grinned and then mouthed, "Be nice!"

Begrudgingly taking her advice, he said, "Mrs Dennison, let's start at the beginning shall we? Answer my questions as fully as you can and we'll see where that gets us, alright?"

At her mumbled apology he said, "You say you husband was in Portsmouth the same night of the latest murder?"

"Yes, but he might not have been!"

"Sorry?"

"That's what he told me, but he could have been lying. Just like he was lying today. Just like he's probably been lying to me for years. I can't cope. I don't know what to do!"

Ciaran didn't either, but said, "Please, Mrs Dennison, try and calm down. Where are you?"

"In Reading, outside the shopping centre. I saw him, he's in an Italian restaurant having lunch with someone, but I can't see who it is. I rang his mobile and he told me he was sitting at his desk having a sandwich! So you see, he can't be trusted can he?"

Ciaran was alarmed by her mental state and could hear she was crying as well as gibbering. But Reading was too far away for him to get to her in time, to help calm her down.

"Look Mrs Dennison, are there cafés where you're sitting?"

"Yes, yes there are, lots of them," she gulped.

"Well, go and have a coffee or tea while you compose yourself enough to drive home. Yes?"

"I suppose I could," she sniffed.

"That's great. Once you get home, perhaps you'd like to email me your thoughts about your husband. It's much better to have these things in writing, don't you think? Then as soon as I've read it we can talk again."

"Yes, yes, thank you," Mrs Dennison now sounded like he'd just pulled her into a lifeboat after nearly drowning at sea. But it seemed he'd done the trick.

"I'll text you my email address right now. Okay?"

"Okay." Her previously laboured breathing sounded more natural now. "Thanks again," she said and cut the call.

Ciaran expelled a rush of air and hoped to God he'd calmed her down enough to drive home safely. What was it with women and this investigation? First Donna and now Mrs Dennison getting upset. It appeared his role as a knight in shining armour was in great demand. But it wasn't really the image he wanted to project. It was nowhere near the incisive, decisive, detective he was aiming to be.

Theresa

It was an inane American television programme that had given her the idea. *Private Eyes*. Once she saw it, she couldn't get the equally banal song out of her head, *Private Eyes* by Hall and Oats, which was the programme's theme tune, albeit sung by someone else.

She'd sent the email to DC Douglas as he'd requested, detailing her husband's strange behaviour and had had an acknowledgement. But nothing else. She wasn't a stupid woman. She knew she had to find evidence if she was ever to convince the police to investigate her husband. So, if Tim really was the killer, the one they called 'the Choker', a term that never failed to elicit a shudder through her slight frame and make a hand fly to her neck, then she'd just have to find some. As he rarely left his electronic devices, mobile and netbook, lying around, that line of enquiry wasn't going to work. Oh, that was a good phrase, she decided, line of enquiry. It sounded very detective-like. That train of thought clinched it. She was going to pursue a different line of enquiry, by following her husband.

The trouble was she didn't know when something might happen, when another killing may take place.

Thinking about it logically, as she did the ironing in the kitchen, if he was to murder someone it would be at night, so perhaps she should just follow him when he was supposed to be working late at the university, or away at a so-called speaking engagement. That's when he was more than likely lying.

Putting down the iron and wiping her face, as she'd become hot from the steam - please God don't let it be the start of an early menopause - gave her another idea. She'd more than likely be following him at night, but she still wanted to ensure she wouldn't be recognised. So she'd have to change her appearance. A wig and glasses should do it, she decided. There wasn't much she could do about the car, but both of their vehicles were quite popular models. As long as she didn't park under a street lamp or anything, she should be okay.

She thought back to the episode of *Private Eyes* she'd seen. They seemed to spend an inordinate amount of time sitting in cars and watching and waiting for something to happen. So it didn't appear she'd hit on a clue, or evidence, the first time she followed him. But, she reasoned, if she didn't start, then she'd never find anything out at all. Whilst the two private eyes were waiting around, she'd noticed they detailed comings and goings in a diary. At last she'd have use for that new empty one she had. She anticipated filling it up quite quickly.

As she finished ironing the last of Tim's shirts and hung it on a coat hanger, she wondered where she might buy a wig. A hairdresser? No she'd not seen one in any of the local salons. What about a department store? Debenhams? John Lewis? Yes, it would have to be somewhere like that, so it was time for a trip to The Oracle again. Oh and glasses with plain glass in them.

She mustn't forget those. Maybe her opticians would have an old pair of frames she could buy. She could always tell them it was for a fancy dress party.

Grabbing Tim's shirts, she bounced up the stairs. Opening his wardrobe she pushed the other coat hangers aside and plonked in the new ones, hooking them quickly over the bar without bothering to even up the hangers, or sort the shirts in colour order, as she would normally do.

She was a woman on a mission, she decided as she got changed, uncharacteristically leaving her discarded clothes on the floor of the bedroom. She was going to prove once and for all that she was more than a stupid housewife, who only had the cleaning to fill her time. She'd show DC Douglas she was intelligent and highly motivated. Who knew, perhaps she could get a job in a police station? They took on loads of civilian staff these days, at least according to the telly. She'd have experience of evidence gathering and surveillance to put on her application form.

Grabbing her handbag, Theresa flung open the front door so hard it banged against the opposite wall. Giggling she pulled it closed behind her and headed for her car, singing as she walked up the drive, *"Private Eyes are watching you..."*

Crane

Holly and Ciaran staggered into the CID office, carrying two large boxes. Huffing and puffing they reached their desks and put their load down with a thump.

"You two alright?" called Crane.

"Oof that was heavy. Why can't people use laptops at work? It's got to be more convenient than tower systems," said Holly. "And these bloody things have come out of the Ark!"

"Money, I expect," said Ciaran. "If they aren't broken, why fix them? Or rather change them in this scenario. They're the work computers from Sally and Charlie's offices," Ciaran explained to Crane. "They've just arrived downstairs and Holly couldn't wait for someone to deliver them, so she roped me into helping her cart them all the way up here."

"So what are you hoping to find?" he asked Holly.

"Any social media accounts that aren't on their phones or laptops. It suddenly occurred to us," she smiled at Ciaran, "that maybe both Charlie and Sally wanted to keep their involvement in a dating site away from any of their friends or family. And the best way to do that would be to use a work computer instead of a personal one."

"Wouldn't the companies notice?"

"Not necessarily. They both worked in large offices. It's too time consuming to have someone monitor everyone's internet usage all the time, especially if they regularly log on for work, so most firms don't bother."

As Holly got her head around connecting the towers to her spare keyboards and monitors, leads and connectors growing like weeds under her desk, Crane and Ciaran turned to the only other lead they had, the Suzuki Jeep seen on the CCTV camera from the multi-story car park near to where Charlie lived.

"So, how many have we got, boss?"

"Too bloody many, son," said Crane, who had been in this situation many times before. It was easy to get bogged down trawling through large information dumps, but it had to be done.

"Let's see if we can find a way of narrowing down the search parameters."

Crane and Ciaran had been at it for about an hour, changing the search criteria in terms of colour, location, male owners, female owners when Holly shouted, "Yes!"

Grinning Crane said, "I take it you've found something?"

"Bloody right I have. Oh, sorry, guv," she mumbled sheepishly. "Anyway," she continued brightening up again, "They've both got S-Dates accounts!"

Theresa

That morning, as he'd kissed her goodbye, Tim had a small grip bag with him and said, "Oh, sorry, forgot to tell you, I've got a meeting at Southampton University tonight, so I'll be leaving Reading about 5pm and I'll stay over down there, or in my room at Reading. Okay?"

When she didn't respond, he said, "Right oh, see you tomorrow night then," kissing her on the cheek.

She tried hard to not flinch when he kissed her and hoped he'd not noticed her shrinking away from him. She didn't want him to think there was anything different about her. Over the past few days Theresa had been very busy, purchasing the things she needed for her stake out. As she closed the door behind Tim, she was thrilled that at last she had a reason to follow him. Now it was just a matter of getting ready. She couldn't pass up this opportunity. Racing through the housework as she still had her standards and wasn't about to let them slip because her husband was a potential murderer, at last she was finished and free to get ready.

She practised putting the wig on, tying her long brown hair up and placing the wig so none of her own hair showed. It took several attempts, her fumbling fingers not as sure as those of the saleswoman in the department store where she'd bought it. She ended up putting it in a low ponytail and then draping the end of it up onto the top of her head, fixing it with grips. That way she didn't have a large bump in the back of her head. The short blond wavy hair transformed her face, bringing out the slight rosiness of her cheeks and warming her skin tone. Looking at herself this way and that in the mirror at her new persona, she seriously considered having a complete make-over, once this was finished. Perhaps she'd become stale and ordinary, as time had passed by. It looked like her determination to keep her hair long hadn't been the best stylistic decision after all.

The glasses, which she wasn't entirely comfortable with, tended to end up perched on the end of her nose, giving her a slightly quizzical look. She wasn't keen on those at all and vowed if her eyesight ever went, she would definitely get contact lenses or even have laser treatment.

She completed her outfit with soft black flat shoes, dark leggings and a comfortable large sweater, mindful that it might be cold at night and she might not be able to keep the engine running for the heater.

Into a large shoulder bag she put her diary, which was no longer pristine and clean and empty, a paperback book she was reading, several pens and pencils and a pencil-sized torch, before going downstairs to find a small cool bag for her sandwiches and the big thermos for lots of hot coffee.

Settling down at her laptop she then proceeded to find out as much about Southampton as she could, never having been there before.

She read about how Southampton was the largest city in Hampshire with the university being one of the major employers in the region. She got bogged down in the history of the place and had to tear herself away from tales of Henry V and his famous warship HMS Grace Dieu which was built there, turning her attention to a map of the city which was far more relevant for her.

Not sure what time Tim would really be leaving Reading, she made her way over there in the early afternoon. Finding a discreet parking space in the street near to the exit of the car park where he always left his car, she sat back in her seat, adrenaline coursing through her body. She was so keyed up she didn't know what to do with herself. She tried reading, but every few words she heard a car and had to glance up to make sure it wasn't Tim. She got out of the car, but was afraid to walk too far from her vehicle in case he drove off and she lost him. She drank a cup of coffee, but that made her jitters worse.

At last she saw his car nosing out of the car park, waiting for a few cars to pass before a space opened up. Throwing everything onto the passenger seat, she turned the key to start her own car, very glad she'd left the key in the ignition as she doubted she would have been able to get it into the slot as her hands were shaking that much. Gripping the steering wheel, she let a couple of cars go past her, before she pulled out. As she kangarooed up the road, she berated herself for her nervousness, telling herself to pull herself together. Then she clamped her mouth shut as she realised she was talking to herself.

By the time they hit the A33 on the way to Basingstoke, she'd calmed enough to settle down and began to enjoy the experience. Once on the M3 she remembered it was a straight run through to Southampton. If Tim really was going to the university, there were three ways he could go. He would either take the early exit onto the A27, or alternatively follow the M27 and come off at Junctions 4 or 5.

The rush hour traffic was upon them and with lorries and vans thundering past her, she became frightened and confused. She was by now only getting occasional glimpses of Tim's car and as she approached the road leading to the A27 she had no idea whether he'd taken it or not. Unable to get into the correct lane herself, she was swept along with the traffic onto the M27. Fighting her way off the motorway at Junction 4, she pulled over as soon as she could and parked safely.

Her breathing was ragged and she was acutely aware she was on the verge of sobbing uncontrollably and losing it completely. She fumbled with the seat belt catch and throwing it off her shoulder, she pushed open the car door and tumbled out onto the grass verge, breathing in what she'd hoped would be fresh air and ended up being nothing more than exhaust fumes, which made her feel even sicker. Bending over and retching she wondered what the hell she thought she was doing. Once the wave of nausea had passed she gulped down a small bottle of water, which helped clear the foul taste from her mouth and ease the headache that was threatening behind her eyes.

After a while, she felt able to return to the car and determined not to admit defeat just yet, she made her slow way to the university campus intending to drive around in the hope of seeing Tim's car. After two hours of touring the city and the university she finally admitted defeat. Faced with at least an hour's drive back home she felt it best to get something to eat. Spying a fast food outlet next to a petrol station she pulled in.

Sitting down and munching on a piece of chicken she

mulled over her experience of being a private detective. Her scalp itched from sweating under her stupid wig. She'd long ago ditched the idiotic glasses and her diary was empty as she had no information to write in it. All she'd managed to do was lose Tim at a crucial time, given herself an anxiety attack and spent a small fortune.

Oh well, she thought, as she cleaned up her mess at the table, she doubted anything would happen that night anyway. At least she fervently hoped it wouldn't.

Boy

Lately I've become obsessed with the fairy tale of Rapunzel, a beautiful girl locked up in a tower with everything she could wish for. Everything, except another person. Dame Gothel shuts her away in a tower in the middle of the woods, with neither stairs nor a door, and only one room and one window. When she visits her, she stands beneath the tower and Rapunzel lowers her long golden tresses so she can climb up them.

I thought it would be fun to try and re-enact the tale. My girlfriend has a bedsitting room, where she lives alone, so last night I stole her keys while she was sleeping, left the room and locked her in. Oh, I took her mobile phone and her laptop as well.

All day I have been so excited. I couldn't concentrate on my A level coursework. All I could think about was Annabel waiting for me. Locked in. Totally in my power. I kept wondering if she was as aroused as I was. I forced myself to wait until five o'clock. It was exquisite agony.

Because she has short hair, I knew not to go to the window and call for her. So I stand before her door. I slowly put the key in the lock and inch it open. And there she is, lying on her bed. Her eyes-lids flutter open.

"Thank God, you've come back," she says.

I fall on her in my eagerness. She keeps saying something, but I can't quite make out the words and anyway she's putting me off. As she squirms and tries to get away from me, I clamp my hand over her mouth and with the other gather up her arms and pin them above her head, forcing my knee between her legs. This is the best sex I've ever had and I'm not about to let her spoil it.

Rapunzel, Rapunzel, let down your hair.

Crane

It was too early in the morning for Crane's hip. Having been dragged out of bed at 5.00am by a phone call from Anderson and then met at the front door of his house for an hour's drive to Southampton, he'd had no chance to do his exercises and knew from past experience he'd suffer for it.

At last they arrived at their destination and he climbed stiffly out of the car into the early morning mist coating the city. Within moments he was covered in fine drizzle and felt a twinge of arthritis in his hip as it protested at the damp. Oh joy. That was all he needed. He experienced a flare of anger as he tripped and stumbled his way along the pavement. Derek moved closer and grabbed his elbow.

Crane shook it off, hissing, "Don't!"

Anderson stopped walking and began to lag behind him, so Crane stopped also. He couldn't believe he'd just snapped at his friend like that. At the one person who'd believed in him when Crane hadn't even believed in himself, in those dark days after the accident.

As Anderson drew near, Crane said, "Sorry. I was out of order."

Anderson merely nodded and kept walking, leaving Crane to stumble on, unaided, in his wake, fumbling in his pocket for yet another little white pill.

Inside the terraced house, situated in the middle of a small housing estate full of streets of carbon-copied homes, was an all too familiar scene. Upstairs a young woman lay on her stripped bed, tied to the headboard by silk scarves, with a third wound around her neck. To Crane, her expression seemed to convey her surprise at the unexpected turn of what she'd no doubt perceived was going to be a night of safe, if kinky, sex. Anderson told Crane she was Dawn Murray, aged 26. She was single and lived alone.

A discreet cough behind them made Crane and Anderson turn around, on Crane's part a welcome diversion from the sight of yet another beautiful, dead, young woman. He shook his head at the waste.

"DI Anderson?"

Anderson agreed and introduced himself and Crane.

"DI Thomas. I understand you're from Major Crimes and you've a couple more of these murders?"

"Unfortunately, yes. So we'll be working on this as well as your local team. Three bodies means we have a serial killer on our hands I'm afraid."

"Yeah, I've already been told that," he grumbled. "I was told to hand responsibility for the investigation over to you. It seems you're to be Senior Investigating Officer, not me. And I also understand your own pathologist is coming."

"Well, it makes sense, don't you think? He's done the PM on the other two victims."

"Nothing wrong with my bloke."

"I'm not saying there is, it's just that…"

"Has her phone or a computer been found?" Crane

interrupted them, not wanting to listen to the two detective inspectors snipe at each other in the decidedly frosty atmosphere that was building. And anyway his leg was killing him standing up. He needed to get on with the investigation, not stand there like a Muppet.

"Nothing yet."

"What about her car?"

"What about it?" Thomas was becoming more defensive with each question.

"Has it been checked yet?"

"Buggered if I know. Ask the scenes of crime officers. I can't be expected to know everything."

With a sigh, Crane tramped his way back down the stairs, wincing with each step. Reaching the hallway, he spied a set of keys hung on a key hook near the door. Pulling on latex gloves he grabbed them and went outside. A push on the key fob produced a flash of lights and a beep from the Audi on the drive. Opening the door, Crane got a whiff of perfume and air freshener, which made a nice change from the pungent smell of death overlaid with bleach that was pervading the small house. The inside revealed nothing of interest, so he hobbled round to the boot. Again using the key fob he unlocked it. As the lid swung open he was greeted with the sight of a black laptop bag. Grabbing it, it felt satisfyingly heavy.

Turning back towards the house he collided with DI Thomas. Anderson was still with him and Crane grinned at his boss. "Looks like we've a laptop. Our killer didn't find it as it was in her car. He's getting sloppy, which is good for us."

"I've got people who can look at the laptop," DI Thomas said holding out his hand.

Crane looked at Anderson.

"Thanks, but we'll take it back to our technology specialist, just as soon as we've logged it into evidence." Anderson's tone brokered no dissent and Thomas turned and stalked back into the house. Crane imagined him to have smoke coming out of his nostrils and pawing a foot on the floor. A bull of a man, acting as his bulk suggested.

Both men were glad to get away from Southampton and on the drive back to Aldershot Crane noticed Anderson looked washed out and seemed to be having trouble keeping his eyes open.

"You okay?" Crane was concerned for his friend. "You're beginning to look as ill as I do. Want to stop for coffee?"

"No, my stomach feels too upset after seeing yet another dead body. I'd more than likely take a smell of the coffee and run for the toilet."

"I just thought it might help keep you awake."

Anderson turned to glance at Crane. "Do I look that knackered then?"

"Yeah, you do. Shame I can't drive with this bloody gammy left leg."

"I've been thinking about that," said Anderson.

"Oh yeah?"

"I've managed to get a pool car for the team's use. Or rather for your use as it's an automatic. So next time we go out we'll take that and you can bloody drive for once!"

Theresa

For a while Theresa luxuriated in the feeling of having the double bed to herself. Dappled sunlight came through the muslin curtain and all that could be heard was birdsong and the sound of a lawn mower. Some eager beaver, up early, was doing the gardening. Her expedition last night had left her exhausted and she'd collapsed into bed, being dead to the world for, she glanced at the clock, oh wow, a good eight hours. After one last stretch she got out of bed and after visiting the bathroom, padded downstairs to put the kettle on. Decaf tea, she thought, I've had far too much coffee lately.

On the kitchen table was evidence of her nocturnal wanderings; the cool bag containing the sandwiches she'd not eaten and the empty flask. The wig lay like a small cat curled into itself on the chair and her large bag was slung over the back of the other chair, the unread paperback hanging halfway out of it. Theresa grabbed the lot and dumped it in the bin.

Realising what she'd done and retrieving her handbag and double checking it, she saw her purse was in there, which she rescued, but she decided the rest of it could go, diary and all. She just wasn't cut out to be a private eye, or female sleuth, or whatever the hell they called them these days. It was by turns too stressful and too boring and too expensive a pastime, which had led her absolutely nowhere. Anyway, she had a more pressing problem. She decided the kitchen needed cleaning again. There were water stains on the draining board, and she could see a scattering of crumbs where she'd missed the bin when dumping her uneaten toast yesterday morning. That was something she could control. A situation she could change and more importantly, make better. Once she'd had her tea, she'd better get to it.

Wandering into the front room, holding her mug, she stayed standing and picked up the television remote. Clicking it on, the familiar face of the breakfast programme presenter was relaying the headline news story. As Theresa watched transfixed, the mug slipped out of her fingers and fell to the floor, cascading scalding hot tea in its wake.

It was the burning on her legs that brought her round and she yelped at the pain. Running into the kitchen she grabbed a couple of tea towels. Hopping from one leg to the other and squeaking, she returned to the lounge and put a tea towel down on the carpet to try and blot up the tea and then running back to the kitchen, rinsed the other under the cold water tap. After squeezing it out she returned to the television, sitting down on the sofa and placing the cool, damp towel against her hot skin.

She had to wait ten minutes before the headline story was repeated, during which time she stared at the flat screen on the wall, afraid to take her eyes away for even a moment, just in case she missed the piece again. She was sure she'd just heard a third body had been found. Another victim of the Choker. A young woman dead. This time in Southampton.

Holly

Holly's eyes had lit up at the laptop brought in by Crane and Anderson earlier. Her fingers were flying over the keys. But she didn't seem to be getting very far.

"Please, please," she kept muttering as she grappled with cracking the machine's password. Charlie's password had been found on the list taped to his computer desk. Sally's had been relatively easy to find out as she'd used her surname. But Dawn's was proving slightly trickier.

"Ciaran," she shouted.

"I'm only here, Holly," he admonished.

"Oh," Holly looked up and saw him sitting opposite her. "So you are, sorry. Can you just pass me the file you've got on Dawn Murray, please?"

"Having trouble?"

"Just a tad. But it's nothing I can't handle," she said defensively.

"I know, I know, chill. Here it is."

"Thanks, and um, sorry," Holly said before she buried her nose in the file. There weren't many things she couldn't crack and she wasn't going to be beaten by a password. Most people used names of family, pets, houses, work, mates etc., as passwords. And if numbers were required as well, they tended to use their house number, or date of birth, or even their National Insurance number. It wouldn't take long, she was sure of it.

She'd already poked around a lot in Sally and Charlie's S-Dates accounts. So far she hadn't found any friend matches on both those accounts, but there were a few people that Sally, at least, had become rather involved with. She didn't really expect to find details of liaisons, she was sure their killer was more sophisticated and mindful of laying a trail than that. No doubt any further chats would have been moved to other means of communication and the telling private messages deleted as soon as they were read.

She was counting on the company behind S-Dates giving her details of any users she identified as being of interest to them, thereby falling under suspicion in a murder investigation.

"Come on!" she shouted as she succeeded in unlocking the laptop and there on the home screen of Dawn's computer, was the beautiful S-Dates logo.

Looking up she saw the DI, Ciaran and Crane walking towards her desk.

"Oh, sorry," she said. "I shouted that out loud didn't I?"

Ciaran nodded. "Well?"

"Dawn has an S-Dates account."

"Thank God for that," the DI said. "Right, get on that first, Holly. I want a full search warrant request pulled together as soon as possible with names of users we are interested in. He must bloody well be in there somewhere, it's the only point of reference we have so far between all three of them."

Holly had every intention of 'getting on it' as the DI had put it. She didn't need to be told. But putting her bruised ego aside she smiled and said, "Yes, guv."

"In the meantime," he said turning to Crane, "you and I need to fashion a press release about the third victim and I think we'll also release the fact that this S-Dates app thingy is common to all of them."

"So we can ascertain if other users have been approached for this type of sexual pleasure through the site?"

"Exactly."

The DI was telling Ciaran to continue with the search for Suzuki Jeeps as Holly tuned out their voices and dove once more into the shark infested pool that was S-Dates.

Aldershot Mail Online

Local Murder Update

Aldershot Police have issued an update on the murder of local girl Sally Smith. They have revealed she was a member of the dating site S-Dates. Billed as the 'go to site' for sensual and sexual encounters, police believe this might be how Sally met her killer. No further information was forthcoming, despite repeated questioning by this newspaper. We have been drawing comparisons between Sally Smith's murder and the killing of Charlie Keating in Portsmouth, and Dawn Murray in Southampton, but are still awaiting official confirmation there is now a serial killer on the loose in the Hampshire area.

Needless to say we urge all our readers to stay away from S-Dates for the foreseeable future, until the Major Crimes team find this sadistic lunatic. However, if anyone has met someone through the S-Dates site that wanted sex involving auto erotic asphyxiation, then please contact the team via Crime Stoppers on 0800 111 222. They would be happy to hear from you and you could be doing your community the greatest service of all, by helping the police find and apprehend a serial killer.

Theresa

Even though she was expecting him, the scraping sound of Tim's key in the door made her jump and a small, "Oh," escaped her lips. Clamping her mouth shut, she continued scrubbing the pans in the sink.

"Hi," he called from the hall.

"I'm in here," Theresa managed to reply.

Tim ambled into the kitchen, his hands in the pockets of his corduroy trousers and peered over her shoulder.

"What are you doing?"

"What does it look like? I'm washing the pans." Theresa passed the back of her hand over her hot forehead, pushing away tendrils of hair that were sticking to her clammy skin.

"Um, Theresa, they're clean now."

Theresa lifted the one she was scrubbing out of the hot soapy water. Peering inside it she said, "No, there's still stuff stuck on the sides."

"I can't see anything."

"Well I can and it's why I do the cleaning and washing up and not you," she said, banging the pan down on the drainer.

Seeing the look on Tim's face made her realise he'd

not seen her clean lately, as she normally had everything done before he arrived home. But after learning of the third murder that morning, this time in Southampton, the need to clean the house had been stronger than ever. Once that was finished, she'd decided to check all the pans in the cupboard, after needing one to make a curry and had found them in a terrible state. But she hadn't kept track of the time. Hadn't realised the day had slid by without her really noticing.

Grabbing a tea towel to dry the pan and her hands, she said, "Sorry, I got a bit carried away," and tried a smile, but was sure it came out more of a scowl, as she was having difficulty looking at her husband, never mind meeting his eye. "Anyway the curry is ready, as is the rice. Just let me just pop some bread into the oven and I'll come through."

Tim looked at her askance but left the kitchen as she suggested. He returned in a few minutes with a glass of red wine.

"I thought you might need this," he said putting it down on the kitchen table, then left her alone once more.

Jesus, she'd have to be more careful, she thought, as she grabbed the glass and took a larger than normal swig, which made her cough instead of calming her. But how to appear normal was the conundrum. For she had no idea what normal was anymore.

Going through to the lounge, she was relieved to find Tim engrossed in his netbook, so she turned on the television and watched a quiz show for ten minutes until the bread was ready. She was very glad of the silence and at the lack of conversation.

Over their meal, eaten in the kitchen as she'd never got round to laying the table in the dining room, Tim rambled on about his evening in Southampton. Talked about some social sciences study that was being done about policing and young people, which was apparently the whole point of the meeting. Theresa doubted this was true. Not that she doubted the study was real. It was just she sensed the meeting was fabricated. Either that or it could have been a meeting that had taken place at some other time.

At last, Tim pushed away from the table and declared he was stuffed. "I fancy a bath," he said.

"Go on then," Theresa said, trying not to sound too eager to have him out of the way, although she was. "I'll clear up."

As she stacked the dishwasher she heard his footsteps overhead, the taps being turned on and then, finally, his exclamation of relief as he lowered himself into the hot water. Moving as quietly as possible, like a jewel thief after a prize, she entered the lounge, leaving the door open, so she could still hear Tim splashing around. Her target was his netbook. She doubted it would still be there. But it was, on the seat of the chair and open.

She knelt down, facing the netbook nestling on the seat. The screen was dark, but as she clicked the space bar, the screen lit up. She'd often seen Tim put in his password, but had never known what it was. This time it wasn't needed. The screen revealed his desktop. Nestled in between the icons for Word, Adobe and his internet security provider, was a symbol she had only seen once before. On the television news. It was a large capital S with smiling faces peering around it. It was the S-Dates logo.

Theresa tried her best to stifle the scream. She stuffed her fist into her mouth and practiced the technique for controlling her breathing, whilst gnawing on her knuckles. In - two three, out - two three, in - two three, out - two three. Then she stopped and took her hand out of her mouth, afraid she was going to be sick.

Scrabbling away from the chair, she managed to get to her feet and backed away from the netbook as though it were a ticking bomb about to explode. In fact, that was a pretty fair approximation of how she was feeling - as though her life was about to be blown to smithereens.

She was afraid to go anywhere near it. She was afraid of what she would find if she clicked on the logo. She was afraid if she touched anything, Tim would know. And punish her for it. If he could kill others, then he could kill her. The thought made her sway on her feet.

She glanced at the telephone. She could call 999. But then when they asked what her emergency was, she wouldn't really know what to say. Please come and arrest my husband, I think he's a killer but I have absolutely no evidence whatsoever. Yeah. Right. That would work. She audibly sighed. Then looked up, just in case Tim had heard her from the bathroom. That wasn't likely, she berated herself. She had to try and hold it together.

Still backing away from the small laptop, she found the sofa and sat down, her legs no longer able to hold her up. She sat on her hands to try and stop them trembling. She supposed she could ring the young detective; he'd always been nice to her. Not that he'd believed a word she'd said, but at least he'd never actually laughed at her. Glancing at her watch she saw it was 9pm. He wouldn't be at work now. Didn't the detectives work during the day? She thought so, at least from the television programmes she'd watched.

Finally realising she was on her own and facing a night of sleepless terror, she did the only thing she could think of. As she walked upstairs, doing a pretty fair impression of a zombie, she met Tim on the landing.

Swathed in towels he looked at her, a frown furrowing his brow. "You alright, love?"

"No, must be a migraine or something. Thought I'd take some tablets and go to bed."

"Good idea, you look rather pale. And didn't you say you'd been cleaning all day? You shouldn't work so hard. I keep telling you that."

Theresa just about managed to mumble some sort of acknowledgement of his words and stumbled into the steamy bathroom. Opening the cupboard on the wall, she found her sleeping pills. On the odd occasion she'd used them, she'd only taken one. Sometimes it had worked quickly and other times it hadn't. She needed to make sure this time, so she shook two tablets out of the tube and swallowed them with water cupped in her hands from the tap.

Once back in the bedroom, she ignored the damp towels Tim had left all over the bed, just glad that he wasn't still in the bedroom. Stripping off, she let her clothes fall to the floor and climbed in under the duvet. Shaking uncontrollably, as though she had a high fever, she waited for sleep to claim her.

She could hear a buzzing sound. It had woken her up. She waved a hand around her head in case it was an insect. But it didn't help. The buzzing persisted. Her eyes fluttered open. As the light hit them and her pupils contracted, she groaned. What had she done to her head? She felt as though she'd been on a giant alcohol bender, something she'd not done since her student days. She had a headache that felt like Thor's hammer was pummelling her skull. She squinted in light as harsh as in any desert. Her mouth felt as though she'd completely and utterly dehydrated and had not one ounce of moisture left in her body. Then she remembered what she'd done. It was the sleeping pills. It seems she shouldn't have taken two after all.

But the good thing about it was she had slept through the whole night and into the next morning. She put out her arm and felt the space behind her. Tim wasn't there. Thank goodness. The buzzing had stopped. It must have been her mobile phone. At the moment she couldn't cope with reading any message, or returning any phone call.

She swayed with the vertigo that gripped her as she stood and made her grope for the furniture. It took several minutes for her to get downstairs and once in the kitchen she fell on a bottle of water from the fridge, downing it in one. The water helped clear her head a little and she decided the next thing she needed was caffeine.

Turning to the percolator she found a piece of paper propped up against it. It was from Tim.

Didn't want to wake you. Hope you're feeling better!

"Not really," she said to the cheery note. "And I won't do until you've been arrested." Crumpling it up she put it where it belonged - in the bin.

Despite her fumbling fingers she managed to get the coffee maker going and while she was waiting for the restorative brew to percolate, she padded into the lounge and put the television on. But she'd missed the breakfast news programme and was treated to one about doing-up houses. Snapping it to the 24 hour news channel she turned up the volume and went to get her coffee.

But it seemed the media had moved on to bigger and better stories since yesterday and there was only the smallest of items about the murder in Southampton, which merely said the police were still looking for clues as to the identity of the killer and anyone with any information should contact the Major Crimes Unit at Aldershot. They were particularly interested in hearing from anyone who had experience of the dating site S-Dates.

Thinking that contacting the police was very good advice indeed, she climbed the stairs with the aid of the bannister and went to get dressed. Her limbs were still heavy and her brain fuzzy from the sleeping pills, but she managed to dress herself in jeans, a tee-shirt and a jacket and look reasonably respectable.

But driving was altogether another matter. She ended up crawling along at 30 mph from her house on the outskirts of Reading to Aldershot, her hands clamped to the steering wheel, a journey which should have taken half an hour and ended up being nearer an hour.

Managing to park in the small shopping centre car park she had to stop and buy a bottle of water before she went to the police station. Jesus, she mustn't do that again, she thought. She hadn't realised how potent the innocuous little pills were. No wonder people who wanted to commit suicide took them. A mouthful of those and you'd definitely go to sleep and never wake up.

Anyway, back to the matter in hand. She now had to persuade someone to listen to her. And, more importantly, believe her.

She walked into the building housing Aldershot Police Station with its drab, grey, concrete façade and asked for DC Ciaran Douglas, her diary clutched in one hand and her handbag in the other. She'd managed to find the diary in one of the rubbish bags in the bin outside the back door. For once she thanked the local council's policy of only collecting the waste once every two weeks.

"And you are?" the burly policeman on the information desk asked.

"Mrs Dennison."

"Can I tell him what it's about?"

"I've got information on the murderer."

"Which murderer?"

By now Theresa was beginning to feel she was being interrogated herself. Just like a suspect would be.

"I didn't know you had more than one," she said rather stuffily. "The one called the Choker."

"That's a term used by the press, not the police."

"Well, whatever the hell you call him, I want to see DC Douglas. Now are you going to tell him I'm here?" Theresa had risen to her full height, which was still considerably shorter than the man in front of her and therefore not at all intimidating.

"Wait over there," he said indicating a row of plastic chairs fixed to the wall. "Please?" he sighed as she refused to move until he'd asked nicely.

"Very well," she said and did as she was bidden.

Actually she was rather glad to sit down. She'd begun to sway and didn't want the officious policeman to think she was drunk, or on drugs, or something. She needed to be taken seriously.

While she waited she sipped her water, hoping it would make her feel better sooner rather than later. She needed to keep it together while she talked to DC Douglas.

It was a little over fifteen minutes before he appeared. Walking over to her he said, "Sorry, Mrs Dennison, but I can't see you at the moment, I'm on my way out."

Theresa panicked. "Oh please, it won't take a minute. It's about my husband." She felt ashamed to be pleading with the young man, but needs must.

"Again?"

"Yes, again. I've been following him and he's now been in the vicinity on the night of all three murders. Here," she thrust the diary at him. "I've written it all down in there."

DC Douglas took the diary, but she felt he was reluctant, rather than excited by her offering.

"Alright, I'll read this when I get back," he said as he turned, ready to walk away.

"And then there's the S-Dates account thingy."

That stopped him, she saw with some satisfaction, as he turned his attention back to her.

"He has an S-Dates account?"

"Yes."

DC Douglas sat down next to her, the row of six chairs groaning, as they were connected to each other.

"Have you opened it?"

"No, I didn't check his account as I didn't want to take the risk of him knowing that I'd looked at it, as I didn't know how it worked."

"So you don't know his user name or anything?"

Theresa had to admit she didn't.

"Well," Douglas said at the end of her confession. "I still have to go out, but I'll look at the diary when I get back and discuss it with the rest of the team."

"You'll let me know if I can help any further? Or at least tell me what's going on?" She couldn't help pleading with this young man, desperate as she was that he take her seriously.

"Of course," he said. "Well, I'm sorry, but I really have to go now," and as they stood he shook her hand and she watched his back as he walked away, all the while hoping he wasn't walking away from her for good.

Ciaran

The reason Ciaran was rushing away from Theresa Dennison was simple. He was on his way to meet Donna for lunch. They'd arranged to meet in the small shopping centre next to the police station. He'd decided on one of the restaurants, not feeling that the café in the Morrison's supermarket was exactly romantic.

Not that he was feeling romantic towards Donna. He smiled. Well, actually that was a big fat lie. The last time they'd met they'd enjoyed a drink in the bar in Donna's hotel. He could easily have made a move then. But he'd restrained himself. She was floating in a sea of insecurity and anxiety and he wasn't about to make her feel even worse by frightening her with an unwanted advance. She was struggling with her flat mate having been killed by someone she'd known, or at least had agreed to meet for sex, so it would have been incongruous for Ciaran to put Donna in a similar position and one she may have considered dangerous.

He was aiming to make her feel secure, by being there for her. As long as she didn't end up seeing him as a brother. Heaven forbid. That would be awful. Maybe he'd best take a small step towards a romantic relationship, before he blew it altogether. He just wished he was more experienced in these matters. He'd had a couple of girl friends at university, but they hadn't been the focus of his attention. He'd been far more interested in the course he was taking and that had therefore consumed most of his time.

He quickened his stride as he caught a glimpse of her sitting in the cordoned off area outside the restaurant. When he arrived, the sight of her took his breath away. She'd ditched the work make-up and her skin glowed, her eyes sparkled and her mouth creased into a smile. As she rose to her feet he took the opportunity to give her a kiss on both cheeks and a slight hug. His skin tingled where she'd kissed him back and if he wasn't careful he'd end up with a goofy grin on his face for the next hour. Hiding behind the menu gave him a chance to pull himself together.

Once they'd been served, he decided to talk about the case and said, "I'd meant to ask you, did Sally mind you going away so much?"

"Not at first," said Donna, putting down her knife and fork. "But she started to talk about it over the past few months, I think."

"Why?"

"Well, she'd broken up with her long-term boyfriend and hadn't had one since. So she really was living alone there, whereas before he'd stayed over a lot when I was away."

"Did she do anything about extra security?"

"How do you mean?"

"Extra door or window locks? An alarm system perhaps?"

"No," Donna shook her head. "Not that I remember and I suppose I'd have noticed if she had."

"Yes, I suppose you would."

"Are you any nearer working out who killed her?" Donna asked.

Ciaran had been waiting for that one. She always asked about their progress. And why shouldn't she? She had never been affected by crime before. But he had nothing new to tell her. At least nothing positive.

"The only thing we have is that a particular car was noticed in the area of the killings."

"What kind?"

He wasn't sure telling her that would help and in fact it was something that hadn't been released to the press yet. But then again, it might not hurt.

Before he could decide what to do she said, "Please, it would help me. If I saw such a car near to my flat I could let you know."

She had a point, he decided, so he took the plunge. Anything to keep her safe. "A red Suzuki Jeep. The model is called a Jimny."

"Thanks, Ciaran," she said and to his surprise she took his hand. "It means so much knowing I've got you to call on if anything happens, or if I get frightened on my own."

Not wanting the moment to end, he covered her hand with his other one. "You can call me anytime," he said. "I'll always be there for you." He wanted to say much more, but he held his tongue.

The waiter interrupted the romantic interlude, which burst the bubble they were encased in and they both jumped a little. Ciaran let go of her hand. Feeling slightly bereft he said, "Do you want anything else?"

Donna looked at her watch. "No, sorry, I'd better go. I've got to go into the office at Heathrow this afternoon and I better get a move on."

Once Ciaran had paid the bill, they manoeuvred their way out into the large plaza.

"Want to meet up again?" Ciaran asked, hoping he didn't sound too beseeching.

"I'm flying again tomorrow, going to the US this time," she said. "But I'd love to see you when I'm back."

Ciaran grinned and decided it was now or never, as he moved in to kiss her. He was still anxious about the proprietary of it all, as she was the dead girl's flatmate, but still, rules were meant to be broken, or at least bent.

As they pulled apart, Donna said, "I'm feeling very vulnerable, Ciaran. I keep thinking the killer will come back for me. It's stupid, I know. I've moved back into the flat but I'm too scared to stay there alone. I was wondering… would you be able to come round tonight?"

Crane

Ciaran had just made his little speech to Crane and Anderson about his short chat with Mrs Dennison and had been dismissed by Anderson, having been told to leave the diary behind.

"What do you reckon, Crane?"

"We've sod all else," Crane grumbled and squirmed in his chair, trying to get comfortable and wondered if he needed to keep a collection of cushions at work. He had one in the car and a load at home. It seemed to ease his injuries if he had a something softer to sit on. Also the slight elevation of his hips helped as well.

"All this proves, though," said Anderson thumbing through the diary, "is that he was in the vicinity at the time."

"Or he says he was. We don't know if he was the first and second times. He could have been lying, as Mrs Dennison openly admits."

"Alright," Derek sat up, seemingly having come to a decision. "Let's have a chat with him."

"What? Call him in for interview?"

"No, let's call on his professional services shall we? I feel the need to consult with an expert, and one that lectures in criminology should be right up our street."

"Hasn't Ciaran a degree in criminology?"

"Yes, but the Professor doesn't need to know that does he?"

"Well you'd better explain to Ciaran first what you're doing and why, otherwise he's going to be a very unhappy puppy."

"What's got into you? Suddenly gone all caring on me have you?"

"No, Derek, it's called professional respect," Crane bristled.

"Jesus! Can't you take a little joke anymore? I'm just pulling your leg, Crane. Let's call Ciaran and Holly in so they know what's going on."

Crane struggled to stand and limped out of the office. After telling Holly and Ciaran to get themselves into the office, "PD bloody Q," he stopped off at his desk drawer and dry swallowed a pain killer. He kept trying to bring down the dose he was taking, but every time he missed a pill he'd get uptight, angry and sullen. He really must get a hold on it all, maybe after this investigation was over. If he wasn't a basket case by then.

They'd managed to arrange to see Professor Dennison at the end of his teaching day. As that was at 3.00pm - mid-afternoon to Crane and Anderson who couldn't get over such an early finish - they barrelled over to Reading University. The Department of Law was on the main campus and by having a chat with a nice parking attendant, managed to get a reserved space near to the building.

Crane was glad of the opportunity to stretch the kinks out of his gammy leg, but he'd only just got into his stride before they arrived at their destination. He was still having difficulty juggling his work/life balance and as a result the physiotherapy exercises he was supposed to be doing were losing their important place in his daily regime. Tina kept suggesting he return to a physiotherapist, for at least that would make him do something about it two or three times a week. But, like a lot of things, he hadn't got round to organising it yet. Maybe when the case was over… Then he realised this was rather becoming his mantra.

A passing student directed them to Professor Dennison's room and Crane knocked on the large wooden door with the handle of his stick. After hearing a shouted something, muffled by the thick door, Anderson turned the handle and they walked in to a large room with mullioned windows, high ceilings and a large rug, whose pattern was mostly undetermined, because of the large number of students' feet that must have crossed it to the desk located by the window.

The Professor stood as they entered and introduced themselves, and they ended up doing an awkward round of handshakes over his desk. Crane half expected the desk to have one of those large embossed leather sections on the top of it, to go with the whole 'this is a traditional seat of learning' vibe, but was surprised to find a large industrial, utilitarian metal one.

Dennison must have noticed Crane's puzzled look, for he said, "My mahogany desk is being renovated and would you believe this was the only spare one I could find? It's bloody cold to the touch and noisy to use," and he demonstrated opening and shutting a drawer with a screech. "But I guess beggars can't be choosers."

Crane thought Dennison looked less like a beggar and far more like the respectable, well-to-do educator that he was, with his soft Viyella checked shirt sleeves rolled up to his elbows worn over a pair of dusty coloured chinos. He reminded Crane of an off-duty army officer, an image which brought with it a pang of regret.

"Anyway, how can I help the police?"

Anderson explained they were with the Hampshire Major Crimes Unit. "Have you heard of our murder cases that have been in the news lately?"

"Ah, the Choker."

Anderson sighed audibly. "Yes, that's what the newspapers and the television are calling him."

"Or her," said Crane, just to be awkward.

"Exactly," Anderson said, throwing a glare at Crane.

"It's best to keep an open mind about these things." That got Crane another dagger look from Anderson, which he took as a sign to keep his mouth shut.

"So why are you here?"

Anderson said, "If I've got it right, criminology is much more than the study of committing crimes; it is the understanding of how crime affects society as a whole from a range of perspectives, including social, historical, legal, political, and psychological."

The Professor grinned, "You sound like our departmental brochure."

As Dennison didn't say anything else, Crane jumped in. "We're particularly interested in the motivations behind the criminal or deviant behaviour displayed by our killer."

Dennison rested his chin on the knuckles of one hand. But still didn't join in the conversation. To Crane it felt like he was employing one of their own police interview techniques on them.

"So we want to know all about the kind of person who would be into breath control play; more properly known as asphyxiophilia."

At last Dennison spoke. "Isn't that more a question for a psychiatrist?"

"He wouldn't be able to give us a social background of such a deviant. We want to know what type of person this could be; we need more than just personality traits."

"So you're thinking of age range, social status, employment, that sort of thing?"

"Exactly," said Anderson. "Can you help us?"

"I'd need access to your files."

Anderson picked up his case and opening it pulled out three slim buff coloured folders and handed them over. "I must ask for complete confidentiality," he said, before he let go of them.

"That goes without saying," said Dennison.

"Not in my line of work, sir."

Crane could hear the steel in Anderson's voice and wondered if Dennison had picked up on it.

"I can assure you of my complete discretion," he said. "I take it this is urgent?"

"Very," said Crane, who was fed up with keeping quiet. "How soon could you give us your professional opinion?" with a hint of sarcasm on the word professional.

"How does two or three days' sound? I'll ring as soon as I'm ready."

"Thank you, sir," said Anderson, passing over a business card and rising from the hard, ladder backed chairs they'd been sitting in. He nodded to Crane, indicating the door with his head.

"What is wrong with you?" fumed Anderson as Crane limped back to the car.

"Well, the pompous idiot reminded me of officious army officers."

"Jesus, I see army bigotry is still alive and well and living inside you."

"He's an academic. He has no idea of the outside world and how it operates. Did you see his jacket? Did you?" Crane pulled open the car door. Banging it shut behind him he turned to Anderson and said, "His jacket has leather patches on his elbows. Can you believe it? I know his sort," and Crane turned away to jerk his seat belt across his chest.

Ciaran

After hours of trawling through CCTV footage from around the murder site in Southampton, Ciaran found something. At last. A fleeting image of a Suzuki Jimny Jeep. He couldn't seem to find it anywhere else other than it exiting the M27 going towards the university. But he did have a partial number plate. He now had the same car in all three locations.

Leaning back and stretching in his seat, he was tempted to go and tell Anderson or Crane about his find, but for once decided to curb his enthusiasm for spreading the good news and just get on with the next task in hand - finding Suzuki Jimny Jeeps with that partial plate in Hampshire. Then he had a thought. The incidents took place in Hampshire, but that didn't mean to say the killer lived there. He, or she, could live in a county close by. That meant he had to widen his search with the partial plate. Looking on a map he'd pulled up on his computer, he decided the killer could potentially live in Surrey or Sussex to the East, Dorset to the West, or Berkshire to the North.

He stilled for a moment. Berkshire. That rang a bell. Reading was in Berkshire. Professor Dennison worked at Reading University. It wasn't beyond the realms of possibility he'd travelled to Aldershot, Portsmouth and Southampton from Reading. Just as his wife had said. A quick search of the DVLA revealed that Profession Dennison had a Honda Civic. Bugger.

He ran his hands through his hair in frustration. It looked like Mrs Dennison was a bit paranoid after all. Oh well, it had been worth a try.

He glanced at his watch. Donna was flying out today, but if he hurried, he'd catch her before she left for the airport. He grabbed his phone and left his desk, smiling at the thought of talking to her again.

Holly

Holly didn't notice Ciaran leave his desk. Deep in S-Dates, she'd managed to find user accounts for two of the victims. She now needed to crack the third. Dawn's laptop had revealed an S-Dates account, but she hadn't saved the password. Holly had tried some obvious ones, drawn from Dawn's life but none of them had worked. But what she had managed to do was to find the email passwords. Dawn had saved them in a word document on the hard drive, so it was a fairly simple matter to request a new password from S-Dates. The email duly arrived and Holly replied to it and changed the password, making a note of it on the file.

That small problem solved, she was now able to access S-Dates, logged in as Dawn and check the private messages. And there it was. An arrangement to meet on the night of her death. She now had three S-Dates accounts, three victims and three arrangements to meet. Her reward for the effort and hours she'd put in to find out that information. She huffed out a breath of satisfaction and allowed herself a small smile. But she knew it wasn't enough. Each meeting had been arranged with a different S-Dates user.

Feeling as though she was taking two steps forward and one back, she realised she had to go back to S-Dates and get access to the personal details of those three users. Ciaran had arranged the search warrants last time, but when she lifted her head to ask for his help again, he wasn't there. He was gone and so was his mobile. Probably off chatting to Donna. Again. She grabbed her own mobile and savagely keyed in a message to him: *Get your arse back here - we've work to do!*

Boy

I hadn't meant to kill her. Not really. It had been an accident. Unplanned. Something that had just happened. Such a pity, I thought, as I looked down at her, sprawled across the bed. She had been so beautiful. Still was. For death had yet to change her.

Colourful silk scarves were juxtaposed with the pale whiteness of her skin; splotches of colour at her wrists and neck. Her button nose had a dusting of freckles on it and her red hair fanned out across the pillow. Her face had relaxed and she now appeared serene, as if welcoming the end. Glad of it. Accepting of it.

We had found each other on the internet and had met purely for sex. A special sort of sex. The type of sex I had wanted to explore for years and had never before had the opportunity. I'd practised on my own, but lately it hadn't been enough. That's when I decided I needed more. A partner to explore with, share with, achieve orgasm with.

She had been the choker to start with, tying my hands to the bed and then placing a silk scarf around my neck. As I'd become aroused, she'd pressed the carotid arteries. I had been able to feel her finger tips pressing into my flesh, the slither of the scarf underneath them. My brain, denied the oxygen it needed and craved, had made me feel giddy and light-headed. As she'd pressed and released, pressed and released, I'd climaxed with a rush of pleasure, the like of which I'd never before experienced. As I'd fallen back, gasping, I'd felt like I'd gone to Heaven and back.

Then it had been my turn to be the choker. And that's when I'd felt the real power. The power of life and death over her was like nothing I'd ever known. My hands had tightened on the scarf, pulling it against her neck, denying her brain oxygen - the basic element of life. Her eyes wide, and unable to speak, she'd silently pleaded with me to stop.

But I didn't stop.

Couldn't stop.

Wouldn't stop.

Not until she'd collapsed. Her eyes no longer imploring. No longer seeing.

It had blown my mind.

Crane

Crane watched as a young WPC escorted Professor Dennison to their meeting in Anderson's office. He was looking around the incident room with unbridled interest, which made Crane decide on a strategy he could use later on. He was particularly interested in the Professor's reaction to their investigation and findings to date. But all that would come later. For now he intended to watch the man closely.

Dressed in casual chinos and shirt again, Crane noted the Professor wore his clothes well. Upright and confident, he commanded attention, but not in a showy way. The four of them stood as the Professor entered the room. It was with a quiet aura of authority that he looked around the room and held each person's gaze in turn, as he shook their hands. Holly and Anderson smiled a friendly greeting, but Ciaran's grin seemed more reminiscent of pulling a face while sucking a lemon and Crane noticed his handshake was limp and quick.

As the meeting started, Crane focused on the Professor, who reached for his briefcase and drew out several folders. He placed these on the table and wriggled a few times in his chair as though to get more comfortable. He leant on his forearms and looked at Anderson expectantly.

"Thanks so much for coming, Professor. We're all looking forward to your analysis of the perpetrator. Aren't we?" After a few mumblings from the rest of the team, he nodded for the Professor to begin.

"Well this was certainly an interesting project for me," he said. "I'd firstly like to thank you for thinking of me and I can only hope my insights may be of some value."

Here we go, thought Crane. A typical academic who uses ten words where one would have done.

"As you have already concluded that the same person is responsible for all three deaths, I haven't bothered with that side of the investigation, rather focusing on the type of person who would have such predilections. I believe that was what you wanted to know?"

"Exactly, Professor," said Anderson.

But Crane was wondering how much longer he could keep his concentration, if the man continued with his convoluted language.

"This particular case has necessitated I draw on not just criminology, but forensic psychiatry and pathology. Using all these tools, I have been able to determine some characteristics for you. Recently, use is being made of 'dynamic' risk factors, such as: attitudes, impulsivity, mental state, family and social circumstances, substance use, availability and acceptance of support. So I've used those to make a structured professional judgment."

Crane caught Ciaran rolling his eyes and had to stifle a laugh.

"Sexual offenders exhibit heterogeneous characteristics, yet they present with similar clinical problems or criminogenic needs e.g., emotional regulation deficits, social difficulties, offense supportive beliefs, empathy deficits, and deviant arousal."

Crane came out of his fug. Perhaps they were getting somewhere at last. He wondered why Anderson was letting the Professor waffle on. But maybe it was a ploy, or a technique, so Crane had better let him be.

"Because there doesn't seem to be research on a type of sexual predator with our man's particular deviancy, I decided to explore the type of person who becomes a rapist, as this is the nearest offender category and has been well documented. In comparison with child sexual abusers, rapists are more likely to be younger, to be socially competent, and to have engaged in an intimate relationship in the past."

"Can I just stop you there, Professor. Ciaran, would you just make bullet points of this on the whiteboard please?"

Ciaran glared at Anderson, but Crane was glad to see he did as he was asked without comment.

"So he's probably a young man, socially competent and has had sexual relationships. Is that right professor?"

Dennison nodded and then continued with his lecture. "In addition, rapists often display the following criminogenic needs: intimacy deficits, negative peer influences, deficits in sexual and general self-regulation, and offense-supportive attitudes."

Crane just had to interrupt. "I get the gist of what you're saying, Prof, that our man finds intimate relationships difficult, he's been around others of his type who have influenced him possibly such as the BDSM community and he finds it difficult to control his needs. But 'offence supportive attitudes' has me stumped."

Professor Dennison smiled at Crane, "To simplify it, our man justifies his desire for auto erotic sex by seeing it as being a perfectly normal sexual desire. He doesn't think it's wrong. Furthermore he feels entitled have to his own particularly strong sexual desire. He wants and needs it, so therefore he can have it."

"That's all a bit cold and callous," said Anderson.

"But it rather sums him up, doesn't it, Inspector?"

"Christ," muttered Holly.

Dennison said, "It almost goes without saying that he is a prolific internet user."

"Nothing goes without saying," countered Crane. "Please assume we know nothing and tell us everything. That way we won't miss out on a potentially critical trait that would help us to catch this monster."

Dennison didn't seem at all offended by Crane's bluntness. He just dropped his eyes to his papers and carried on. Perhaps he saw Crane as an annoying student, a thought that made him smile. Then he quickly had to re-arrange his features into something more solemn as Dennison continued.

"There is a group of sexual offenders who use the internet as part of a pattern of offline contact offending, including those who use it to acquire victims and/or disseminate images that they produce."

"Sorry, you're losing me," said Anderson.

"I think what Profession Dennison means, is some predators migrate from seeking and finding images on the internet, to meeting with actual, real people, with whom he can bring his sexual deviance to life. The internet is therefore used to find victims as well as providing a source of images which could provide him some sexual satisfaction," said Ciaran from his position by the whiteboard. "Hence his membership of S-Dates."

The Professor looked mildly surprised and said, "Exactly, thank you for that succinct explanation,

Detective. So, let's look in more detail at our man's possible background. We should expect to find experiences whilst growing up of physical abuse, parental violence, emotional abuse, and cruelty to animals."

"Ah, said Holly, "the whole setting animals on fire sort of stuff."

"Precisely. These experiences can result in externalizing behaviours. As an illustration, researchers have found physical and verbal abuse during childhood leads to antisocial behaviour and callous personality traits, both of which lead to aggressive sexual fantasies. So, an individual who has been raised in an emotionally impoverished environment is often unable to identify his emotions in an accurate manner and, as a result, is likely to become confused when confronted with emotionally charged situations. These individuals often react to confusing situations with overt aggression."

Crane watched Anderson nodding his agreement and wondered if he was as confused as Crane was.

"I think he frequently masturbates, which suggests problems with emotional self-regulation. Frequent masturbation coupled with frequent pornography use, increases the likelihood of sexual compulsivity. Likewise, insecure attachments suggests; intimacy deficits, empathy deficits, antisocial lifestyle, and social difficulties. Violence in the home has been shown to be predictive of antisocial lifestyle, a hostile attitude toward women, emotional callousness, and hostile masculinity.

"Jesus," said Holly. "I'm liking him less and less."

"Individuals who have experienced child maltreatment are likely to exhibit distorted internal working models of relationships, which results in poor social skills and emotional self-regulation. The lack of social skills, especially during adolescence, is likely to result in rejection by others, which in turn will decrease self-esteem, increase anger, and produce cognitive distortions about peers and relationships. Negative emotions combined with those cognitive distortions may increase the intensity of sexual desire and deviant sexual fantasies."

"So basically he's an aggressive sexual predator who thinks he can take what he wants from any woman he meets," said Crane, wondering why the Professor couldn't just have said that in the first place.

"That's right. He's clearly able to carefully plan his offenses and doesn't seem to experience an internal conflict after the offense, because he's achieved his sexual goal."

"Could this impulse to constantly achieve his 'sexual goal' as you call it, have escalated into murder?"

"Oh, must certainly. But more importantly, I believe the taking of life has become an essential part of his sexual deviancy."

Those words echoed in Crane's brain. *The taking of life has become an essential part of his sexual deviancy*. In which case their killer wouldn't ever stop. He wouldn't just have bondage-type sex, or auto erotic sex, he would always want sex that ends with murder. Sex that ends with him strangling the life out of his victim. Crane could see it was a powerful motivator to continue with his killing spree. They had to find him. But how?

Over a welcome cup of coffee, Crane and Anderson chatted further with the Professor, Holly and Ciaran having made their escape, citing pressure of jobs still to do. Crane showed him their incident boards.

"What do you think, Professor?" Crane asked,

showing him the mind-map type diagram that filled one board. The un-named killer sat in the middle of the map with arrows going out to each victim.

"So the only common denominator you have at the moment is the killer himself and a dating site?"

"And the car," said Anderson and pointed to the image of a Suzuki Jeep. "This has been seen on CCTV in the towns where the murders took place; Aldershot, Portsmouth and Southampton."

Crane saw a look of surprise cross the Professor's face, accompanied by a tremor in his hand that made his coffee cup rattle in its saucer. But it was gone in an instant, to be replaced once more by the slightly enquiring look he normally wore. His Professor face, Crane had no doubt.

"Hampshire definitely seems to be his stalking ground," Anderson was saying. "We're having to liaise with the local police, who are aiding the investigation in each of the towns. That's how we managed to get so much relevant CCTV footage. The only trouble is the time it's taking to go through it."

"Don't forget the dating site," Crane said and pointed to the third board, where details of the S-Dates site had been noted. Once more, he caught a faint startled look, before Dennison composed himself. "You know," Crane chatted on, "I never realised how large Hampshire actually was. Are you familiar with the County, Professor?"

"Well, yes, I suppose," Dennison said. "I travel to other campuses quite a bit, so I suppose I frequently visit Southampton and Portsmouth Universities."

"Have you been to either of those recently?" Crane had his 'soldier's face' on. Cold. Inscrutable. Determined. It was as if the temperature in the office had fallen a few degrees.

Professor Dennison put his cup and saucer back on the table and pushed his hands in the pocket of his chinos. "Why do you ask?"

"No particular reason. So, what's your answer?"

"Yes, I've been to both establishments recently."

"Oh, really? When?"

Professor Dennison turned to Anderson. "I thought I was here to talk about professional matters, DI Anderson. Why do you want to know about me? I'm not a suspect am I? I can assure you I don't fit the profile at all." He smiled, but it was one of those grins that didn't light up the eyes.

"You don't fit the profile you've drawn up," said Crane.

Dennison seemed confused. "What are you trying to say?"

Crane paused then laughed. "Nothing, nothing at all, Professor. Anyway if you'll excuse me I have things to do."

Crane grabbed his stick from where it was propped up against his chair and made his slow way out of Anderson's office. He thought it interesting that neither Anderson, nor the Professor, said a word until he'd left the room. Crane definitely felt the Professor had something to hide. His furtive behaviour and his attempts to avoid answering questions pointed to it. But Crane couldn't catch criminals on a feeling, even if it his gut was screaming there was something 'off' with the Professor. He still needed evidence.

Theresa

Theresa was cleaning the silver when Tim came downstairs. He'd been in bed asleep when she'd arrived back from doing a bit of shopping, so she'd left him to it. She was happy to keep their contact down to the minimum, but wondered what he was doing back home before 5.00pm on a work day. Wanting to keep herself busy, to stem the flow of doubt and fear and horror that never seemed to leave her, she'd pulled out the canteen of cutlery and proceeded to clean it.

"Bloody hell, Theresa, can't you find anything better to do?"

His voice coming from the lounge door made her jump and drop the cleaning cloth.

"I'll have you know this is a very worthwhile activity," Theresa said brandishing a fork at him. "Look how tarnished this fork is!"

Tim looked at it askance, then shook his head and walked into the kitchen. "What's for dinner?" he called.

Sighing, she put down the fork and on entering the kitchen watched him looking around. "What are you looking for?" she asked.

"Dinner."

"Oh, really Tim, it's all prepared and in the fridge. We're having steak and chips, so it doesn't need to be cooked until you're ready for it."

"Oh, right, well," he bumbled, pulling a beer out of the fridge.

Theresa looked at him and sighed. Living with such an exacting man was wearing her down. She spent all day keeping things nice and clean and he didn't even notice all her hard work. She looked at her fingers which were grey from cleaning the silver and went to the sink to wash them.

"Did you have a good day?" She wasn't really interested, but it was a topic of conversation and she wanted to chase the scowl off his face.

"I went to Aldershot police station today."

Theresa stopped washing her hands, then realising she shouldn't react, she began again, pushing the soap dispenser plunger and rubbing the soap into them. "Oh really?" she said, still rubbing.

"Yes, they'd wanted my opinion about a case they're working on."

"A case?" Theresa hoped he didn't notice the slight squeak in her voice. She concentrated hard on rinsing her hands under the tap.

"Yes, the one all over the news at the moment."

Dear God. Theresa grabbed the edge of the sink before she collapsed like a marionette, all knocking knees and pointy elbows. "You didn't mention it before." She managed to steady herself, then grabbed a towel to wipe her hands with.

"Well it's confidential, isn't it?"

"So," she mustered what little courage she had and turned to look at him. "Did you help?"

Tim took a long pull of his beer before saying, "I

think so, but all the time I was there, I had this feeling I was being scrutinized. That ex-army chap didn't take his eyes off me. And then there were the questions."

"Questions?" Theresa thought she was going to throw up and swallowed down the bile that had risen up her throat.

"Yes," he sat at the table and so she joined him, grateful for the excuse to sit, as she was sure her legs wouldn't have held her up much longer. "They wanted to know if I went to Portsmouth and Southampton at all, so I had to explain I went to both universities. And then that Crane said something. It was when I said I didn't fit the profile of the killer. I think he was hinting I wouldn't, because I'd written it. I wouldn't write a profile that would implicate me, if I was the killer. It was all very weird."

"He probably meant it as a joke," said Theresa, not thinking that for one little bit. She wished the Aldershot Police had given her a heads up about looking into her husband. She was really very grateful to them, pleased they seemed to have taken her seriously, but she could have done without the shock. Her heart was hammering in her chest like a piston and she could feel pools of sweat gathering under her arms. She had to get away from Tim, get out of the house.

"Anyway, I'm sure it's not worth worrying about," Theresa said. "Why don't we have a nice bottle of red with the steak? Cheer you up a bit." She managed a smile. "I'll go and get one."

But Tim stood up instead. "No you're alright, I'll go. Give me the keys to the Jimny. I'll take your car as it's blocking mine in."

Tim

Despite the steak, which was rather good and the bottle of red wine he'd drunk most of, he couldn't get his brain to switch off. Beside him, Theresa rolled onto her back, her legs tangled in the duvet, and began snoring. That was all he needed. The bloody woman drove him mad. No wonder he stayed away so much. They just didn't seem to have anything in common anymore, not since the children had grown up and left home. He had seen it as an opportunity to try new things, meet new people and to live a little after the years of struggling to bring up the boys. No matter what anyone told you, children changed your life big time.

He was finally enjoying his life. Being true to himself. Home was just somewhere to sleep now. To rest and recharge his batteries. Before his next foray into a world he'd never known existed in his previous, boring, life. With Theresa still sounding like a pig on heat and most of his side of the duvet wrapped around her twitching legs, he decided a cup of tea would do nicely and shrugged on his dressing gown and went downstairs.

The kitchen was the warmest room in the chilly house, the heating having clicked off hours ago, so he set up his laptop there and made a caffeine free tea. He was wired enough already. The first thing he did was to pull up his calendar. He needed to double check some dates. The dates when the murders had taken place. As he toggled between his report to the police and his calendar, it soon became clear why the police had been looking at him so closely. During the first murder in Aldershot, he'd been at a conference in a hotel nearby. The Portsmouth murder fitted as well, and his latest adventure in Southampton had been at the same time as the most recent killing.

He was also worried about the car. He couldn't remember which vehicle he'd taken to Portsmouth or Southampton. Even though the Jeep was supposedly Theresa's car, they both used whichever one was last on the drive. It made more sense than keep shunting them backwards and forwards along the thin strip of concrete that only held two cars, end to end. So he could have been driving the Jeep on those three occasions. He just didn't know. Had no way of knowing, really. If he'd left any parking tickets or petrol receipts in there that would prove his location on a certain night, Theresa would have thrown them out by now. She was becoming manically clean and tidy these days. Out of control. Behaving strangely. Hell, perhaps she was beginning to suspect him? Of what, he didn't know. But it would explain the bizarre woman who'd replaced his wife.

His fingers jerked on his keyboard, sending the calendar app out of control, so he closed it down and snapped shut the lid. He'd been planning to go on S-Dates to find his next liaison, but that was before he'd confirmed to himself the police were actually looking into him. Why else would they have wanted to consult him? He'd never worked with Aldershot Police or the

Hampshire Major Crimes Teams before and at first he'd wondered why they'd picked him. But his professional pride had told him it was because he was a leading figure in criminology, at least within the South of England, so it was natural they should contact him.

How stupid and blind he'd been. He should have been far more prepared when he went into the police station today. What would he have done if they'd arrested him on the spot? What would Theresa and the kids think? His face burned with shame and his innards coiled like a python, constricting his stomach and he murmured with the pain. Clutching the table he got unsteadily to his feet and just about managed to get to the downstairs cloakroom before his red wine and steak fed the toilet, instead of giving his body the essential nutrients it contained.

He staggered out of the cloakroom by holding onto the door frame, and trembling and shaking, he knew he'd get no more sleep that night.

Holly

The screen blurred before her eyes and Holly sat back and decided she needed a rest. She had been drilling down the owners of Suzuki Jeeps with the partial plate caught on CCTV. Now that the search had been expanded to counties bordering Hampshire, there was a lot more data to trawl through. Searches only got her so far and she then had to check out each one the computer spat out. She was just going to ask Ciaran if he wanted a coffee as she was going to make herself a green tea, but his phone rang. One look at his face suggested it was a call he'd been waiting for. Donna, no doubt. She hadn't told anyone else he was seeing Sally's flatmate. She wasn't sure if there was a regulation against it, at least until the case had been closed, but doubted if Anderson or Crane would deem it appropriate. She didn't care who he saw, really, but this blossoming relationship was having an adverse effect on his work. Like now. He'd buggered off to talk sweet nothings to Donna, so she couldn't go and get herself a drink, as one of them should to be at their desks, if at all possible. She didn't expect dying of thirst would be reason enough to vacate her post.

Pissed off and with nothing else to do to pass the time

until he returned, she went back to work and looked at her screen again. It showed the search for Suzuki Jeeps with the partial plate in Berkshire. She'd just finished the names A-C and was going to start on the D's after her short break. Idly looking at the names, one of them caught her eye, causing her to sit up in her chair. Dennison, Theresa with an address in Reading.

All thought of a drink forgotten, she shouted to Crane, "Guv, got a minute?"

Crane looked up from the report he was reading. "Sure, come on over."

"No, I need you here."

"For Christ's sake, Holly. Must I?"

"Please, sir, it's important. I need you to see what's on my screen. I can hardly believe it."

"Just tell me, Holly and stop with the theatrics."

Bloody hell. Crane must be having a bad day, she thought. She wasn't the only one who had noticed the change in Crane on what were becoming known around the office as his 'bad pain days'. She really was trying to be sympathetic and understanding, but in truth was getting rather fed up of being snapped at.

"I've found the owner of the Suzuki Jeep we're looking for. It's Professor Dennison's wife. Is that important enough for you, sir?"

Anderson

Overhearing the conversation, Anderson came out of his office. Crane was on the phone, which had rung immediately after Holly's sarcastic comment. He said to Holly, "Did I just hear right?"

"Yes, sir," said Holly. "It's definite. The partial plate matches Mrs Dennison's Suzuki Jimny Jeep."

"Bloody hell." Anderson scratched his head. "I wasn't really expecting that."

"You won't be expecting this message either," said Crane limping over to them. "Professor Dennison is downstairs. He says he wants to talk to us."

"Christ, you don't think he's come to confess do you?"

"Who?" said Ciaran, joining the three of them.

"Where have you been?" grumbled Anderson.

"Call of nature, sir."

"It was a bloody long one," said Anderson, smiling inside at the lad's embarrassment. Ciaran really had to learn to keep his face impassive. Perhaps Crane could give him a lesson or two later on. Right now they had a more pressing problem.

Once Holly had explained to Ciaran what was going

on, Anderson said, "Right. Let's see what he has to say, Crane."

"In your office?"

Anderson smiled, relishing the idea of getting the Professor on the back foot immediately. "No, in an interview room I think. Let's make this a bit more formal shall we?"

While Holly arranged for the Professor to be taken to a free interview room, Anderson went to get his files and Crane a fresh notebook out of his drawer. Holly then printed a still photo from the CCTV they had of the Suzuki Jeep and handed it to him as they left.

Crane stumbled getting into the lift and Anderson said, "You alright?"

"Great. Fine. Never better."

"Liar."

Crane glared, eyes flashing, but said nothing.

"I saw you take a pain tablet just now."

More silence from Crane who seemed focused on his stick.

"You need to get that sorted you know. I've noticed you have bad days."

"And how would you know?"

"Because that's when you're in a bloody awful mood. Now I don't know if it's because you're trying to come off the tablets and suffering withdrawal symptoms, or if you're not taking enough to help get you through the day while you're working. Either way, fix it."

Crane glowered and hissed, "Yes, sir."

"Fuck off," Anderson grinned, treating his friend's comment as sarcasm. Although he didn't believe it was. Not really. "But I mean it, Crane. You can't carry on like this. So until that tablet starts to work, keep your mouth shut in the interview room. The last thing I need is you kicking off at our prime suspect."

"Who me? As if I would."

"Yes you bloody would and you know it."

Anderson's lecture ended as the lift doors opened and they were engulfed in the maelstrom that was the front of the police station. Drunks, pimps and whores were slumped in the seats along one wall. An addict, clearly high, was arguing with the uniformed constable on the desk, who appeared grateful for the reinforced glass he was shielded by.

"Where's our man?" Anderson called.

"Room 4."

Glad to leave the rumpus behind, they walked down the corridor towards the interview room holding Professor Dennison. Anderson had a spring in his step, as it finally looked as though they were getting somewhere.

Professor Dennison was sitting at a grey metal table and jumped up at their entry into the room.

"Professor," Anderson and Crane nodded their hello's and invited him to sit again. "So, what can we do for you? Have you come up with any other insights we should know about?"

"Um, no, not exactly." The Professor squirmed on his chair. "It's, um, about, um…"

"For goodness sake," burst Crane. "Get on with it, man."

Glaring at his friend, with an 'I told you to keep quiet' look, Anderson then turned to Dennison and said, "Please, Professor. We're very busy."

As though the Professor had just remembered who he was, he puffed out his chest and sat upright. "I believe you're looking for a Suzuki Jeep with a partial plate number BD51."

Anderson said, "That's correct."

"Well, it might be my car, or rather my wife's car," he quickly corrected himself. "Our number plate is CD51 SAC."

"And why would the vehicle have been in the vicinity of the murder site in Southampton that night, Professor?"

"Because I was visiting a friend at the time."

"A friend?" Crane butted in.

"Yes, Sgt Major, a friend."

"And who might this friend be?"

"I'd rather not say at the moment," Anderson watched as Dennison lowered his eyes and stared at the table.

"What about your wife?"

Dennison's head snapped up and Anderson was pleased to see he was keeping the Professor out of his comfort zone, with questions outside the scope of what he'd no doubt rehearsed.

"Perhaps you can explain this?" Crane said and slid a photograph across the table.

Anderson sighed. Crane clearly didn't take orders very well. Anderson knew it wasn't out of disrespect, but merely because Crane had been used to being in control for many years. It was clearly a habit Crane was struggling to break. Or was he struggling? Maybe he had no intention of moderating his behaviour. Realising he was wool gathering Anderson looked at the Professor, who didn't seem to be handling the shock of seeing his wife at the steering wheel of their Jeep very well.

"Oh my," he whispered.

"Oh my indeed," said Anderson. "We'd already found out your wife owned the Jeep we were looking for before you came here. And that she was driving it on the night in question. A clever member of my team managed to enhance the image of the Jeep and you can clearly see its Mrs Dennison driving."

"I came in voluntarily," interrupted Dennison.

Anderson ignored his interruption. "So what we need to know from you is what was she doing there?"

"I haven't the faintest idea," said Dennison. "I don't know what to think. Surely she can't be involved? Can she?"

Crane

After leaving the interview room, Crane and Anderson went to the viewing room, to spy on the Professor, wanting to see his reaction to Anderson's words, now he was on his own.

"He looks like those World War One shell shock victims, doesn't he," said Crane, shuffling around to get his stick in the right position to keep him comfortably upright.

"He didn't ask for a lawyer," mused Anderson.

"He's not been arrested though has he? That's when most people run for cover under the safe umbrella of legal advice. And it was his wife driving the Jeep, not him."

"Suppose so."

Anderson still looked thoughtful and the Professor still hadn't moved. Irritated by the whole thing Crane said, "Do you believe him? That he was with 'a friend' in Southampton?"

"To be honest I've no idea what to think any more."

Crane, preferring to verbalise his introspection said, "But why would his wife be going on at us about him, if it's her who is the killer?"

"To throw us off the scent? Misdirection and all that?"

"Is it possible the killer is a woman? Mrs Dennison? Jesus. This is a weird one." Crane's words were as confused and jumbled as his thoughts.

That brought a smile from Anderson. "I thought our previous murder case with DS Bullock at the centre of it was weird, but I think this one tops that."

"So what to do now?"

"A chat with Major Martin, I think."

"On the phone?" Crane said, pulling his mobile out of his pocket.

"No, I fancy a trip out, get some fresh air. We can take your new car."

"What about the Professor?" Crane fumbled as he put away his phone and found the car keys which were lurking at the bottom of his trouser pocket.

"I think he could do with some quality reflection time, don't you? He'll still be here when we get back. Maybe by then he'll be more willing to speak to us."

"But he could just leave!"

"I know that, you know that, but does he know that?"

"Of course he does, he studies criminology."

"Yes, but I'm betting his sense of fair play and 'doing the right thing' will make him stay. Come on, perhaps Major Martin can advise you on your pain medication as well."

Grumbling under his breath, Crane followed Anderson out of the room. Anderson was so bloody infuriating. But he was also the only friend Crane had, and his boss, so he'd better rectify his problems pretty soon. Could he really sort out his pain meds? Could he really continue working, or would his disability make it impossible?

Holly

At last. As Holly checked her emails, the one she'd been waiting for had arrived. S-Dates had eventually sent them the information they'd requested through the search warrant. Careful not to upset the owners of the site, Ciaran had only requested details of the accounts they were interested in. The three accounts that had arranged a meeting with their three victims; Sally, Charlie and Dawn.

Holly wasn't at all happy with the concept of S-Dates. Their tag line of 'sexy, sensual and satisfying encounters' smacked of prostitution. She could understand the more traditional internet dating, where lonely people were searching for their soul mate. From what she could see, it could work pretty well. She personally knew several people who'd had good experiences from such dating sites and met their long term partners.

But just meeting someone for sex? Christ, you could probably pull any red blooded male off the street and offer to meet just for sex. Physical contact, without any of the messy emotional wants and needs that so often went with it. She figured most men would be up for it, the unintended double entendre making her laugh.

But this was no laughing matter, she knew. Three people were dead because of that site. Three young people, not much older than Holly herself, who had hopes and dreams and a future they thought stretched out before them. What had possessed them? Why would they join such an organisation? Why not a more conservative dating agency? Was it really because they wanted sexual deviancies that wouldn't be tolerated by normal partners? Whatever 'normal' meant these days. Specialist agencies like this pushed the boundaries of decency, bringing out into the mainstream, fetishes and BDSM sex. She wasn't naive enough to think such things didn't exist, bubbling under the surface of the thin veneer of respectability. It was just she hadn't encountered them before and she couldn't help but wonder what sort of people the participants were.

Being the type of person she was - inquisitive, driven and compulsive - she'd researched autoerotic asphyxiation in her quest for background information. Historically, the practise was documented from the early 1600s. It was first used as a treatment for erectile dysfunction and impotence. The idea for this most likely came from subjects who were executed by hanging. Observers at public hangings noted that male victims developed an erection, which sometimes remained after death (known colloquially as the death erection), and some occasionally ejaculated when being hanged. Although ejaculation occurred in hanging victims after death, because of disseminated muscle relaxation, there were AEA devotees who felt it happened as a result of the restriction of oxygen to the brain. So really it was nothing new. It had been practised for hundreds of years. Somehow the thought didn't make her feel any better.

Neither did the information from S-Dates. From

what she could see, her fingers had been working frantically whilst she was musing, all three email accounts were now closed. There had been no hits on her searches for the three user names and all the direct messages associated with those accounts had been deleted. All she had left were IP addresses. What were the odds that they were all from cafés, or even libraries, with free Wi-Fi? Pretty high. At least it would give them an approximate location; country, county and town. The location of the IP addresses associated with each account could help triangulate an area where the killer lived, or worked, or at least visited a lot.

Scrolling down through the email from S-Dates it seemed each account had used several IP addresses which would give them even more information. Unless the killer was using a proxy, hiding their real location behind an organisation that cloaks your IP address by bouncing around the signal. In which case it would take a while longer as they'd have to contact the proxy company, which would take another search warrant, which would take another few weeks that they didn't have the luxury of.

Once the IP addresses had been fed into the locator, Holly went to make some herbal tea, thinking perhaps camomile might calm her down. She was feeling rather excitable, which meant she was becoming hyperactive, which wasn't good news. She could feel her heart rate and breathing quicken as she became more anxious about finding the truth. It was the least she could do for the victims. But inducing a manic episode wouldn't help anyone, so she used breathing techniques and her mantra to return to a more centred state.

She was still controlling her breathing when the results of her IP address search came back. Every one of them belonged to a proxy. Shit. More delays. It was time for more drastic action. But would her plan be given approval?

Crane

"So, how are you feeling?"

"Set up," grumbled Crane. He was sitting in Major Martin's office, alone with the doctor. "Going to buy biscuits, my arse."

Crane was referring to Anderson's trip to the hospital shop for biscuits, leaving Crane and the Major sat in the doctor's office in the bowels of Frimley Park Hospital.

"Well, maybe a little. But my question still stands."

"Fine. Great. Never better."

"Rubbish."

Crane's head snapped up from his study of his hands which were holding his stick.

"Your eyes are bloodshot and there is purple bruising under them. You're clearly very irritable …"

"You don't say."

"See. That's what I mean."

"I'm normally like that."

Major Martin laughed. "Touché. Are you eating?"

"Not so much, can't seem to face it."

"Tremors? Shaking?"

"You'd bloody shake leaning on this thing all the time," Crane brandished his stick.

"What's your morphine dose?"

"Supposed to be twenty milligrams three times a day."

"Supposed to be?"

"I'm trying to come off them. So I only take one if I really need it."

"Ah, that would explain it."

"Explain what? Look, do we have to do this? I've got questions for you about our killer. This is just wasting time."

"If you're not functioning correctly, then you're the one that's wasting your time, Crane, not me."

"So now all of a sudden you're a pain expert."

Crane tried to stand up, but failed when his leg buckled, so he fell back down into the chair and threw his stick on the floor. "Fuck this. I've had enough of it. I can't do it. I must have been stupid to think I could."

"Can't do what, Crane? Work? Or come off the tablets?"

"Both, I guess. Anyway, what would you know about it?"

"I am a medical doctor, Crane. I'd like to go through your medication with you and see what I can do to address your addiction to opiates and find different ways to control the pain."

"You can prescribe stuff?"

"You really are being a bit slow today, aren't you? Yes I can. I wouldn't offer otherwise. I also do one day a week at my local GP surgery. So, will you trust me to help, Crane? We've been friends long enough for you to realise I only have your best interests at heart. Now, give me your list of medication."

Once Crane had done that, the Major pulled a prescription pad out of his briefcase. "I'll log you onto the system when I go to the surgery tomorrow, so this will all be documented and legal and in future you can come to the surgery in Ash."

"Ash? Where I live?"

"Yes, Crane. That's where I work, every Friday."

"I never knew."

"You never asked. Now, this is your problem. Prescription painkillers stimulate the reward system of the brain and release a flood of a neurotransmitters called dopamine. Like all commonly abused drugs, opiates in the form of prescription painkillers, are known to stimulate areas of the brain which are associated with pleasurable feelings. Therefore, alongside analgesia, they give you feelings of happiness and the sensation that all is right with the world."

"So?"

"So I need to replace the morphine with something else that works in conjunction with your other painkillers to help control the pain and control your moods."

"Are you talking about anti-depressants?"

"One in particular. Triptizol has been known to work really well in these cases. Now, it will take some time for it to kick in and you might experience increased drowsiness at first, but trust me, it will really help. I'll also slightly increase your Lyrica, which works directly on the nerve pain you are experiencing from your hip. My guess is because you've returned to work there is increased strain on the sciatic nerve, it's become inflamed. Now, this might not work right away," Major Martin finished scribbling and handed Crane the prescription. "But it should start to relieve your pain. And remember, if it doesn't, come back to see me and we'll play around with the dosage a little more. I'll be honest, it's a case of trial and error until we find what works for you, but it will be worth it in the end. I also think you'll benefit from a good multi-vitamin and mineral complex. I'll talk to Tina about that and about your diet. So, will you trust me on this?"

Crane nodded mutely, unable to trust himself to speak. The kindness and understanding of his long-term colleague had made him emotional and the revelation the major viewed Crane as not just a colleague, but a friend, had knocked him sideways. The hard-nosed Sgt Major Crane had to blink away a sudden urge to cry. He was fed up of being emotional and fed up of being in pain. At the moment the pain was in control, not Crane, and which was a new experience. Crane was always in control. He clearly hadn't known how to handle this new and puzzling change in his life. He could only thank God that someone else did and that Anderson had noticed his suffering and known what to do with the knowledge.

"Ready, Crane?" Anderson called from the door.

"What about the real reason we came?"

"That was the real reason, you idiot. Now get the car keys out and let's get back. Ciaran is pulling in Mrs Dennison. I reckon we've got some questions for her as well as her husband."

"I might just have a plan," said Holly, catching Crane and Anderson before they went in to see Mrs Dennison.

"Go on, then," said Anderson. "Let's have it."

"Right, we know our killer makes up false identities and email addresses and uses them on S-Dates. He wants to lure anyone who is willing to take part in a bit of autoerotic stimulation. From looking at the site in more detail, he's looking for 'chokers' and 'gaspers'. He doesn't seem to mind whether his victim is male or female, he's basically looking for anyone up for it. So, I thought we could set up a false identity and pose as someone looking for something a bit different in the way of sexual encounters. That will be me. If we get a suitable response, we could arrange a meeting and catch him in the act."

"Absolutely fucking not!" exploded Crane, not caring that Anderson was the boss. There was no way one of the team was putting himself, or herself, in harm's way.

"But why not? Two of the three victims were female and all three were wanting to meet people who were interested in BDSM."

"So you want to pose as a woman interested in that sort of thing?" interrupted Anderson.

"Yes. I've compiled a profile of what the three victims put out there; ages, hair colour, where they live, access to a flat or house alone. I'm sure I can write a profile that could lure our killer."

"Maybe you should have been a criminologist coming up with that sort of social background information," said Ciaran.

But Crane could see something in his eyes. Was it jealousy? It certainly didn't seem to be respect. But it was about time Ciaran put up his own theories about the killer and the victims. So far he'd been very lacking in that area. Some days he just seemed to be going through the motions. His mind wasn't really on the job and he was far more interested in his mobile phone than he should be.

"Let us think about it," said Anderson "In the meantime we've got to talk to the Professor and Mrs Dennison. You never know it might not be necessary to go to such lengths. But thanks for the idea and the offer, Holly. Come on, Crane, let's go and see Mrs Dennison."

Crane followed his boss as requested, but could see

Holly was pretty fed up as she flounced back to her desk and sat down hard on her seat. But at least she'd had the good sense not to get angry at the boss.

Boy

We simply know each other as the choker or the gasper, depending on the role we are playing. The internet makes you that way, all the made up names, the truths that turn out to be lies and stories invented to impress. But Sally, aka Miss Mischief on S-Dates, had turned out to be who she said she was; young, free and single. I got the feeling she had been lonely, from the way she was so eager to chat via private messages and was logged into the forum night after night.

I'd known she had a flat mate. Sally had said she was an airhostess on long-haul flights and was absent from home more often than not, but she was due back the day after we met. That had helped with my sorrow over her death. Knowing she wouldn't be lying there, alone, for very long.

The trouble was, even though I felt a lot of remorse for killing Sally, I couldn't get out of my mind what had happened. What I'd done to her.

Murdered her.

Killed her.

Strangled her.

It didn't frighten me. It thrilled me. I kept fantasising

about doing it again. In bed, when I closed my eyes, I relived the evening time and time again.

I prevaricated for ages. Could I do it again? Could I kill another girl? In the same way? To start with I decided I couldn't possibly. I wasn't a killer. I was ordinary, not made that way, surely?

I wished Daddy was still alive so I could have asked his advice. He'd have known what to do. After all, I think he killed Mummy. One morning when I came down for breakfast, she wasn't there. Daddy said something about she had to go on a trip. It must have been a long one, for she never came back. After a while I stopped asking where she was and when she would return. It was just Daddy and me. He said it was a good thing she'd gone, because it meant we could live our lives the way we wanted to. And anyway, we only needed each other.

After all the introspection, I came to the inevitable conclusion that it had been the most explosive, mind blowing sex I'd ever had and that my body was crying out for it again. More and more often. In that moment of clarity, I realised I was hooked.

Hooked on the power, the lust, the rush.

I had a sexual addiction, just like a smoker needing one more cigarette, or an alcoholic a glass of wine, or a druggie a snort of coke.

I remember thinking, thank goodness for S-Dates, turning once more to my laptop.

S-Dates for sexy, sensual liaisons.

Crane

"Ah, Mrs Dennison," said Anderson as they entered Interview Room 5. "Thanks a lot for coming over. We appreciate your co-operation, don't we, Crane?"

"Absolutely," agreed Crane, sitting down next to Anderson, the two men now opposite Mrs Dennison.

"Well, I wasn't left with much choice," she spat. "That young detective of yours didn't make it seem like a request. It was more of an order."

"Oh dear, just the exuberance of youth, I expect," soothed Anderson.

But Mrs Dennison didn't look consoled. "Anyway, what's going on? Are you going to arrest Tim? Isn't he the man you're looking for? That murderer? That Choker?"

"I'm afraid there's not enough evidence at the moment, Mrs Dennison."

"Not enough evidence?" her strident voice rang out in the room, reminding Crane of Hyacinth Bucket in the 1990's sitcom. "What on earth are you talking about? Don't you believe me? Haven't I given you enough information?"

"I can assure you it's not a case of whether we believe

you or not, it's a case of having to prove it with proof that supports your claim, such as CCT footage, that sort of thing."

"So what am I supposed to do now?" Crane could see the bluster was draining out of her and she was becoming a rather small, frightened woman. "Just go home and pretend nothing is wrong?"

"What you do or don't do is your affair entirely. We can't advise you what to do, that's your prerogative. But in the meantime, we have some questions for you."

Crane didn't think that had come out quite as sympathetically as he'd intended it to. His bloody army speak was getting in the way again. The formalities of speech he'd used for twenty-two years were proving hard to shake off.

"Questions? Of me?"

"Yes," said Anderson opening his file. "Now, can you tell me where you were on the dates of the murders? And," he slid over a photograph, "what were you doing in Southampton on the night of the latest murder?"

Mrs Dennison had gone very pale indeed. In fact so pale that Crane called for a glass of water for her, followed by a restorative cup of tea, with lots of sugar in it. As she gulped the water first, she haltingly began to tell them what she'd been up to.

"Dear God, woman," said Anderson. "You've been playing private detective."

"Yes, I'd come to imagine I was some sort of private eye, you know like on the television."

"You do realise you've compromised our investigation don't you?" said Crane, all sympathy for the stupid woman gone.

"Why? How could I have done that?"

"Because, if we are to believe your story, any sightings

of your Suzuki Jeep we were counting on as evidence in the case we might want to bring against your husband, is now worthless. Both of you were driving around the same cities at the same time but in different cars. The Suzuki Jimny Jeep we've been trying to trace is yours, but we've no way of knowing from the majority of the footage who is driving the car, you or your husband."

"It's going to be a case of, 'he said, she said'," complained Anderson.

"Exactly," said Crane. "So thank you, Mrs Dennison," Crane looked at Anderson who nodded, "that will be all for now."

"So I can go now? Go home?"

"Yes," Anderson stood and collected his paperwork.

"How?"

"I beg your pardon?"

"I've no car here. Can someone take me?"

"I'm afraid we're very busy just now, trying to unravel this mess. I suggest you use public transport, or take a taxi."

Anderson stormed out and Crane limped behind him, thinking Anderson had just got his revenge for Mrs Dennison leading them up the garden path.

Passing Interview Room 4, Crane could see the Professor was still waiting for them. "What do you reckon?" he asked Anderson. "Should we push him further, or let him go?"

"Let him go. I can't be bothered with either of them at the moment. There is another possible way we can catch him, if he really is our killer."

"Holly's idea?"

Anderson nodded. "Yes, but modified a bit."

"Alright," said Crane and went and had a quiet word with the Sergeant on the front desk, asking him to tell Mr Dennison he could leave and that if he hurried he could catch up with his wife and give her a lift home.

Back in Anderson's office, he and Crane continued to chew things over, metaphorically and literally with a couple of chocolate biscuits with their coffee.

"How about letting the Professor in on Holly's plan?"

Crane spluttered and choked as a piece of biscuit got stuck in his windpipe. After several coughs he managed, "I beg your pardon?"

"We could let him know that we're considering a sting operation."

"But if he really is the killer, he won't show or he won't even respond to her in the first place."

Anderson said, "Granted, but he won't know anything about what Holly puts online, what her contact name is or anything she writes as her hobbies and interests."

"Do you really think he'll carry on killing, even though he knows we're onto him?"

"Possibly, probably. It's an addiction I think. I don't think he can stop. And I think that as a criminologist he would want to show he can get one over on us. Still kill someone even though we're looking at him closely. Show he's cleverer than we are."

"You mean he'll deliberately carry on? So we'd be goading him into meeting someone else and killing him or her?"

"I suppose that's the risk we will have to take."

Crane said, "Well it's a bloody big one if you ask me. Setting him up to try and kill Holly but knowing he might well kill someone else instead, just to show us he can."

"Unless it's not the Professor at all? Or his wife?"

"It could be someone we've not come across before."

"I need to sleep on this," said Anderson.

Crane had to agree. He really could do with some sleep himself. He was getting fed up of the pain waking him up at night and then rarely being able to fall back to sleep until he'd either taken a tablet, or dropped off again a mere hour before he had to get up for work. As he drove home he contemplated what Derek had said about their killer being addicted to murdering his sex-play partners. He clearly wasn't fussy about the gender of his partner, which meant it was the act itself that he was more interested in. Which meant Derek could well be right.

Sitting on the drive of his house, with only the cooling engine ticking for company, Crane tried to put himself in the place of their murderer. He saw again Sally's body, white against the mattress of her bed, soaked in bleach, rendered impersonal, as though the killer had washed away the very essence of her. He shook his head. No, that wasn't what he should be doing. He shouldn't focus on the victim. He needed to see beyond the victim, to the killer himself.

"Tom?"

Crane's head snapped up at the sound of Tina's voice, from where it had been resting on the steering wheel.

"You coming in?"

He nodded and climbed out of the car to join his family. Yes, he needed to get into the head and heart of the killer. But not now. He mustn't let the evil permeate his home. He'd leave his musings until tomorrow, back at the police station. And anyway, he had an addiction of his own to confess to. It was time he told Tina the truth about his problems with the pain and his medication.

The team knew the Chief Superintendent was on his way, when the remainder of the staff in the office fell silent. It was as if Moses was parting the seas. By the time he arrived at Anderson's office the whole floor was quiet.

"What the fuck are you lot looking at?" Grimes shouted, which jump started the room and the normal low hum of worker bees resumed. "Jesus," he grumbled as he entered Anderson's office. "Anyone would think I was a bloody celebrity."

"They're obviously not used to seeing you on the floor," said Holly and Crane watched her face immediately flush red, as she must have realised what she'd said.

"I take it this is your plan," Grimes turned to her. "It would take an outspoken person such as yourself to come up with it. Not frightened of much are you, eh?"

Holly looked him straight in the eye and said, "Not when I see injustice and not if I can do something to change it."

"Anderson, as Holly's senior officer, perhaps you'd like to outline her plan."

If Holly was upset by this very public snub, she didn't show it, Crane noticed. But it was a rebuff for the slight she'd made against him. Fair do's. No leader could be seen to be accepting of disrespectful behaviour, army or police. Strictly speaking, of course, she wasn't police. She was a civilian contractor just as Crane was, but they both had to learn to live with, and work within, the constraints of the system. How tight those constraints were going to be would be revealed in the next few minutes.

After Derek finished speaking there was silence. Then Grimes said, "It's a good plan," nodding briefly at Holly, "and I'm prepared to sanction it, but with one proviso. No physical contact, no meeting anyone."

Crane saw Holly's eyes flash.

Grimes must have caught her look as well, for he continued, "At least not without full support in place and a comprehensive risk analysis done."

"Thank you, sir," she said, a smile playing across her lips, trying to break out from behind the clouds of her bad mood.

"Also," Grimes turned back to Anderson, "I want the Professor put under surveillance. You need to know where he is at all times. Put a tracker on his car and try and clone his mobile phone or whatever the hell it is that you lot do. I want you to know where he is every minute of the day and if you don't, I want to know why not. Understood?"

As they all nodded, Crane said, "I think we should at least track his wife's car and her phone, even if no one is following her."

"Really, Crane?"

"Really, sir. I don't want anyone or anything to give us the slip. At this stage I don't even trust my own wife, never mind his."

As Grimes slipped away down the back stairs, obviously having had enough of mingling with the lower ranks, Crane thought things weren't much different here than in the army. Even the police operated a higher and lower ranking system, and never the twain should meet.

"You okay?" he asked, following Holly back to her desk.

"Yeah, bit of a bastard though, isn't he?"

"He just needs to re-enforce his feeling of being a charge. You know, stroke his ego."

Holly said, "That was a deliberate snub, though, getting the guv to tell him about my plan."

"Look, the only thing you can do is to go along with

it. It's just the system, Holly, it's not personal."

"Well it feels bloody personal."

Crane said, "You need to grow a thicker skin, that's all. You've made your point, the plan is a good one and he's agreed to go with it. You got what you wanted, ignore the rest."

"You think?"

"I think. It'll make your working life here a lot easier. What's that serenity prayer?"

"Something about the wisdom to accept what I can't change and the courage to change what I can."

"That about says it all."

"Alright, Crane, I'll try." As he turned away she said, "And thanks."

He raised his hand in acknowledgement and clumped his way back to his own desk, wondering if he should be taking his own advice.

The chat with Tina last night had gone much better than he'd expected. He'd confessed to his problems with those little white pills and told her about his unexpected meeting with Major Martin. He humbled himself enough to ask for her help. "So what do you reckon?" he'd finished.

"Remember when I had post-natal depression?" she'd said. "I couldn't see I had a problem, but everyone else could. As I see it, this is pretty much the same, Tom. So I'm going to do for you what you did for me."

"Which was?"

"Take charge. Dole out your tablets into one of those little pill boxes from the pharmacy, with the ones you need to take morning, afternoon and at night. I'll go and see the Major, as he suggested and together we can work out a plan to reduce your consumption of the ones that are particularly addictive. As he said, that way you can slowly reduce your dependence but manage your pain levels."

"What did I ever do to deserve you?" he'd asked.

But she'd brushed away the comment. "Stop being maudlin," she'd laughed. "And pour me another glass of wine."

Holly

Holly had done her homework. She'd already studied the online profiles of their three victims and so it wasn't difficult to open an account and write a profile of her own. She filled it with what were known as 'keywords', words from two or three of the victim's profiles. Suggestions of wanting something other than the normal sexual encounter and with her own private space to meet. In the end she wrote three profiles and opened three different accounts with different email addresses. It was laughably easy. All the site host wanted, to be honest, was the money. It didn't even matter that she used the same credit card to pay for all three profiles. She'd submitted everything to the S-Dates site the previous night, and it was with an extra spring in her step that she hurried to work through the crisp morning air, eager to turn on her computer and see her profiles live on the site.

But mingled with her eagerness was a twinge of fear. What if she didn't get any hits on her profiles? What if their killer had moved on to another site? S-Dates wasn't the only company delving into the 'meet for sex' online market. But, she also knew many on-line users had their favourite sites, the one they felt most comfortable with and had begun to have some success with. The balance of probably, therefore, was that the killer would stay with S-Dates. Of course he would. She hoped. Fingers crossed.

Throwing off her coat and then turning everything on, she went and made a green tea whilst waiting for her equipment to warm up. By the time she got back to her desk, Ciaran had arrived.

"Anything?" he asked.

"Fucking hell, Ciaran, I've only just got here."

"Sorry. I'll get a coffee then," he said looking pointedly at her mug.

"You weren't here when I made this," she snapped, revealing her anxiousness.

"Christ, Holly, chill," he said and sauntered away.

Muttering about Ciaran under her breath, who was quickly becoming more of a thorn in her side than a helpful colleague, she logged on to S-Dates, opening the three different profiles on three different machines, so she could monitor them all in real time.

"Jesus!"

"What? Are you alright?" Ciaran spilled his coffee running to her side. "Fuck," he said as he pulled a wad of tissue out of his drawer and mopped the hot liquid from his trousers.

"I've had replies!"

"Yeah, well done, Hols," he grinned, despite hopping around from the hot coffee which had spilled perilously close to his crotch.

"Nearly a hundred."

"Eh?" he said down abruptly. "Never knew internet sex was so popular. How the hell are you going to find our man in all of those?"

"By using the same method she used to write them."

The voice belonged to Crane who had just joined them, surprisingly silent despite his gammy leg.

"Sorry, guv?"

"Go back to our killer's replies and see if anyone has used the same phrases as he did when communicating with Sally and the others. Surely if it worked one way, it will work the other."

A smile spread over Holly's face and without answering she turned her attention to one of her monitors.

"Looks like she thinks it was a good idea," said Ciaran, but he was ignored as well, for Holly was deep into the replies, copying and pasting what she thought could be key phrases, ready to be compared with the huge number of replies she'd received to her ads.

The morning passed in a blur and it was early afternoon before she was ready to talk to the team about her findings. She'd managed to narrow the replies down to three users, and wanted to arrange a meeting with at least one of them. But it was nearly the end of the day before she got a reply from Anderson to her request.

"Sorry, Holly, it's not going to happen," said Anderson.

"What, guv? I thought it had been agreed?"

"It was agreed that Grimes would consider it upon production of a full risk analysis."

"And?"

Anderson said, "And I've done one and he said no. It's just too dangerous."

"Too dangerous for a woman you mean," she couldn't keep the belligerent note out of her voice.

"No, too dangerous for anyone, male or female."

Holly stood. "Well how the hell does he propose we catch this bastard?"

Anderson smiled in sympathy. "That's for us to come up with."

"Bugger this," Holly ran out of the office, turned off her computers and grabbed her bag and coat, ready to leave. She wanted nothing more than to get out of the place where she'd sweated and worried over the case and in the end all that work had come to nothing. She couldn't cope. Slinging her bag over her shoulder she turned to leave.

"Come on, then," said Ciaran, falling into step next to her.

"Come on, where?"

"The pub. I reckon you need a drink."

"I don't drink alcohol."

"Jesus, woman, a sparkling water then," and he grabbed her elbow, steering her through the office towards the lift.

Boy

When I looked back at my memories and previous actions, it is quite obvious I have always had these needs, desires and fantasies. You don't need to be a psychologist to work that one out. I was always happy to be Daddy's Boy, it made me, defined me, made me acceptable in Daddy's eyes. Acknowledging this, and applying the word 'orientation' to my bondage and discipline, sadism and masochism tendencies, has helped me come to terms with my identity.

The BDSM orientation idea cleared a mental path for me. It enabled me to think of BDSM as an inbuilt part of myself. It's in my DNA, making me as individual as my bone structure or eye colour. For years I struggled with it. But when BDSM became something I had to accept, even embrace, it was a hugely liberating way of thinking about it. If I thought of BDSM as an orientation, that meant I didn't have to worry about it or fight it anymore. I had freed myself. I had given myself permission to indulge in my fantasies.

That's why S-Dates is so important to me. They offer like-minded people an opportunity to connect. It's another layer of acceptance, I guess.

Knowing I'm not the only one with these feelings and desires.

Knowing I'm not an outcast.

Knowing I'm not different.

But S-Dates seems to be changing. I can't quite put my finger on it, but there are a number of new people on there who don't quite 'gel'. It's as though they're trying too hard. Trying to be who they're not. I'm avoiding those adverts. Avoiding the ones that have the descriptions off pat.

I wonder if someone is stalking me.

Trying to trace me.

I must be careful.

I mustn't slip up.

Holly

"Feeling better?" Ciaran asked Holly after she'd gulped down most of her water.

She nodded. "Sorry, I was just so frustrated, you know? I've found three possible suspects and I don't get why Anderson won't let the operation go ahead. Will you help me?"

Ciaran suddenly didn't seem so friendly, he shrank away from her and a distrustful look passed over his face. "With what?"

"If I arrange a meeting with one of them, say in this pub, will you be there to watch over me?"

"Eh?"

"Come on, Ciaran. You know I'd do the same for you."

"No, I don't know that, Holly and I don't think you have any idea about the danger you'd be putting yourself in. Because for the sting to be any good, we'd have to catch him in the act. It wouldn't be illegal to meet you for a drink in the pub, a liaison set up on S-Dates."

"Look, after I meet him, all I'm asking you to do is to follow us to my flat."

"All? And what would that achieve? Can you image

me telling Anderson, 'Oh, by the way, guv, I watched Holly go into her flat with her killer and did nothing'? Yeah, that would go down really well. And you'd be dead! For what? No, I can't do it. You can't do it."

"Rubbish," she snorted. "Of course we can. I've got a video camera, one of those nanny cams in my bedroom, so I can film the whole thing."

"What film your death you mean? My God, this is getting worse!"

"Look I'll know it's coming won't I?" she argued. "So I can stop him. Those other victims didn't expect to be oxygen deprived for so long."

"But death can occur after only ten seconds of pressure on the arteries. It's too quick. You wouldn't have a chance." Ciaran grabbed his pint and took a swing. "No, sorry, I can't agree to do this. You must be mad to think I would."

"What about Donna?"

"Sorry? Donna? What the hell has she got to do with anything?"

"Does Anderson know you're seeing her?"

Ciaran stilled. "No, no, he doesn't."

"What do you think he'd say if he knew you were going out with the flat mate of Sally Smith, before her murder has been solved? Who knows what evidence she could be suppressing? Or maybe she's not telling us something that would help the case?"

Ciaran stood. "You bitch. I thought you were my friend. But you're not going to blackmail me. The answer is still no. You can tell Anderson whatever the hell you want, but I won't be party to your death."

Holly watched Ciaran as he shoved his way out of the pub. What she really wanted to do was to throw her glass at his retreating back, but sense prevailed and she had to make do with running most of the way home to get rid of her anger and frustration.

Once home, as she didn't drink nor do drugs, she had to make do with a bit of yoga to try and calm her and then some meditation. Although, if she were honest what she really wanted to do was to smoke a joint and just drift off to sleep. But her drug use was in her past. She'd been clean for too long to mess up her body again.

Climbing into bed she caught sight of her nanny cam. It wasn't a deterrent per se, as a burglar wouldn't know she had one. Wouldn't know to stay away. There was no sign on the outside of her building saying, 'Nanny cams in operation'. But, if anything did happen, at least it would be recorded. If the police realised there was a nanny cam in the room that was. Surely they would see the teddy for what it was? After all she wasn't a teddy kind of person. So it would stand out. Wouldn't it? They were becoming more widely used, particularly when families wanted to catch people hurting vulnerable relatives in care homes and hospitals. But also they were becoming more and more popular with women who lived on their own.

Holly sat up in bed. Jesus Christ. What if any of their victims had one?

The next morning Holly was exhausted from lack of sleep. Once she'd got the idea of a nanny cam in her head, she couldn't get rid of it. It suddenly seemed to be the key to the whole bloody case. So she'd tossed and turned most of the night and had been in the office since 7am, waiting for the rest of the team to arrive.

At last Crane and Anderson walked in and she told them about nanny cams.

Anderson said, "Nanny what?"

It looked as if she was going to have to drag them into the 21st Century, so she explained what they were and showed them the one she'd brought from home, after making sure there were no indecent pictures of her on the video it contained. As it was motion sensitive, she normally made sure she only switched it on at night. Last night, once she was decently dressed for bed, she had turned it on and recorded a little piece, to show Crane and Anderson the results.

"I don't recall a teddy bear in any of the bedrooms belonging to our three victims," said Crane.

"That's not all they are disguised in," she patiently explained. "They are in clocks, smiley faces, radios, wrist watches, smoke detectors, photo frames - loads of things."

"So we will have to check all the items in each apartment?"

"Yes, sir, we will."

"Not us," Anderson said and they all looked at him.

"Forensics will have to," he said. "We're not buggering this up by compromising any evidence. Crane, organise that for me would you?"

"So we just have to wait here? Can't we go along as well?"

"Holly, how much work do you have to do?"

"Well, rather a lot actually," she had to admit.

"Exactly. So get on with your job and let the forensic officers do theirs. Don't worry, you'll know as soon as I do if they find anything."

Having to be satisfied with that, Holly went back to her desk.

"Thank you," grunted Ciaran as he passed her, but he didn't sound pleased.

"What for?"

"For not telling Crane and Anderson about my association with Donna. That's what you threatened to do last night. Remember?"

"Actually, I should be apologising to you. I wouldn't have done that, honest. I was just panicking, angry and upset. I'm sorry, Ciaran. Can we pretend it never happened?"

"Maybe, I don't know," he turned to pick up his phone. "You'll just have to wait and see won't you? Like I had to wait and see, all last night, wondering if my career was over before it had even started."

Holly closed her eyes and realised she had a lot to learn about interacting with the members of her team. She spent too much of her time interacting with computers rather than humans. She was beginning to understand humans talked back, whereas her machines didn't. Humans could be hurt by her outbursts, whereas computers couldn't. She hoped Ciaran would come round. She hadn't meant to hurt him, but could see she had. It would take a while to gain his trust again and she berated herself for her stupidity.

Sighing, she logged into S-Dates to see if there had been any private messages on any of the three accounts she had set up, and forced herself to concentrate on the job in hand.

Crane

"Derek," said Crane, poking his head around Anderson's door. "You best see this."

"What it is?"

"A message and a video file from Forensics. Sally Smith had a nanny cam."

"Dear God – Holly was right!" Derek pushed away his chair as he stood. "Get the others, then."

"Um, perhaps we should view it first. It might not be very nice."

"Why, what have they said?" Anderson walked towards his office door, once again trying to tame his wispy grey hair.

"It's a bit like the warning on the telly, a viewer advisement as it were."

"Oh, I'm not liking the sound of that."

"Neither am I," Ciaran added from where he was standing at Crane's desk.

"Never mind all that," said Holly appearing as well. "Let's just get on with it."

Crane could see she was flushed with success, having been right about a possible nanny cam, but was very much afraid she wasn't going to be as happy as she was now, once she'd seen the video. Not if it showed what he was afraid it had filmed.

Crane sat at his desk and played the file, the others clustered around him. The film opened with Sally leading a young man by the hand into the bedroom and they fell on the bed, writhing, kissing and biting each other. Crane felt it was like watching a porn movie, but with a deeper, evil undertone, as the climax to the film wouldn't be great sex, but murder. They watched silently as the man whispered something in Sally's ear. She nodded in response to his words. He then left the bed and presumably the bedroom, returning with colourful scraps of material in his hand.

"The silk scarves," breathed Holly.

Everyone nodded, no one speaking, as if not wishing to break the spell. Only this wasn't some happy ever after Walt Disney Cinderella video, where Sally got her prince.

They still hadn't seen a clear shot of his face, the smiley face that contained the camera being on the wall of the bedroom, facing the bed sideways on and the murderer had managed, albeit unknowingly, to mostly keep his back to it.

Mounting horror was a clichéd way of describing how Crane was feeling he decided, but the longer the video went on, the higher the suspense ratcheted. A quick glance at the rest of the team showed him what his own face must look like. Holly had her hand over her mouth and tears in her eyes. Ciaran looked as though he was going to be sick and Anderson, well he kept closing his eyes, the wrinkles in his face looking deeper somehow. His eyes, when they were open, were dulled by the awfulness of what he was watching.

The murderer, for what else could Crane call him, lay on his back on the bed, allowing Sally to loosely tie the scarves around his wrists and then to the bedpost. Finally she climbed on top of him and slipped a scarf around his neck. Now they could see his face, as he thrashed this way and that in orgasm. But there was no clear image they could use, as his face was contorted in ecstasy.

There was a pause as both caught their breath, then the man sprang off the bed and tied Sally down. Crane noted he used double knots on the ones binding her hands to the bed, whereas she'd only used one knot. That meant he could have easily pulled his hands away if he'd so desired, whereas Sally wouldn't be able to. It appeared Sally hadn't noticed. Her face flushed, eyes wide and body already thrusting up towards his torso, she appeared to be perfectly willing to be tied up. As the scarf slid around her neck she closed her eyes in acceptance of what he was going to do.

Entering her, his face in profile, his hands then went to the scarf on her neck. Placing his hands on either side, he squeezed her arteries with his thumbs, in time with his thrusts. At first glance that seemed enough for them both. Sally was arching her back and gasping great lungs full of air as he released her arteries. They found a kind of rhythm that seemed to satisfy both parties.

But then, without warning, her killer wound the ends of the scarf around each other, enabling him to tighten it against her neck. This was clearly something Sally hadn't bargained on. Her eyes bulged, mouth opened, hands tugged weakly against the scarves binding her hands. But instead of releasing the pressure on her neck, he appeared to increase it, savagely thrusting into her as she struggled against him one more time, then fell limply against the bed, the life leaching out of her body.

Holly cried, great gulping sobs escaping from behind her hand. Crane was glad he was sitting down, but had to grab hold of the desk to stop himself falling off his chair. Ciaran turned and put his arms around Holly, possibly to hold himself up as much as her and Derek held on to the back of Crane's chair as though it were a lifeboat in a stormy sea.

Holly was just about to stumble away, when Crane said, "Wait!" His hand hovered over his mouse. "There!" he shouted in triumph.

Frozen in time was the face of their killer, as he looked straight at the nanny cam and grinned. Just as if he'd known it was there the whole time.

Holly had run to the Ladies toilets, Ciaran had stumbled back to his desk and was sitting there with his head in his hands. It was only the two oldies who were left looking at the image on Crane's computer.

"I expect Holly can get a good still from that," said Crane, unable to look away from his monitor.

"Yes, when she calms down a bit." Derek was still standing behind Crane. Still holding onto the back of his chair.

"I've never seen anything like this before," said Crane.

"Me neither. To see the whole thing laid out before us."

"I know. Every other time we investigate a murder, we have to imagine how it happened. What it would have looked like and how the victim must have felt. But this? No, never this. I've never watched a murder from start to finish."

"I guess there's a first time for everything," said Derek.

"I could have done without the experience."

"Me too."

"Guv?" They both turned to see Holly stood there. She was white faced, red eyed and shaking. "Do you mind moving?"

"Moving?" said Crane stupidly. "Oh, right, sorry."

Crane stood up and shuffled out of the way, while Holly took his place and proceeded to save the image he and Anderson hadn't been able to look away from. Crane realised he was still mesmerised by that face, those eyes, and the look of triumph in them. "I guess that's more or less what happened in the other two murders."

"I'd say so," agreed Anderson.

Holly was still clicking away on Crane's keyboard. "I wonder who he is."

Anderson managed a chuckle at that comment as if to say that Crane was still in la la land and clearly not thinking straight. "That's the big question, isn't it?"

"Right," Holly interrupted them. "I've taken a jpeg from the video. I've sent it over the intranet to our four workstations and I'm also printing several copies off."

"This clears the Professor," said Crane.

"And his wife," added Anderson.

"Yes and his wife."

"So now we have to identify him."

"Holly can run a facial recognition search against the database," called Ciaran. "What about door to door around the three murder sites? Get some uniforms to go back and canvass the areas again, as now we've got an image to show the residents."

"Yes, that will place him in the immediate vicinities, which we'll need to do. But it still won't identify him."

"I'll do a search on social media. See if I can't find his face anywhere," Holly said. Crane looked blankly at her. "Facebook, WhatsApp, profile pictures, Instagram, LinkedIn, you know, all the usual."

Crane nodded as though he understood what she was talking about. Grabbing his stick, he said, "Think I'll just get some air, Derek."

"I think I'll join you."

Once outside, the two of them stood side by side in the car park, surrounded by cars and people, but not seeing any of them. Crane silently smoked a cigarette, noting Derek seemed as dazed as he was.

"What a bloody awful job we do," he said, grinding his cigarette underfoot, wondering if he should have another one.

"Someone's got to do it," said Derek and walked back inside, head down and his hands in his pockets. But the words weren't spoken with any conviction. Crane sighed and followed Derek in. He could wait a while before having another cigarette. Bugger the electronic ones. Nothing replaced a real fag, and if ever a moment had called for one, what they'd just been through certainly had.

Anderson

Anderson, as the SIO, had the dubious pleasure of telling Grimes what they'd found. He approached Grimes' office with leaden feet. Not only had they discovered gruesome evidence, but it seemed their murderer was completely unknown to them. Had they latched on to the Professor too quickly? Had they taken the manic ramblings of a scorned wife too seriously? He wasn't sure. Wasn't sure of anything anymore, including if he wanted to keep doing the job. How many more depraved individuals could he stomach?

When he'd first signed up for the police, all those years ago, he was as eager and gung-ho as Ciaran had been when he'd first joined the team. But the years had dulled that eagerness. Weariness replacing enthusiasm. Age defeating youth. He thought his wife might be glad of the rest as well. Maybe it was time for 'the conversation'. The one she'd been waiting for all these years. Should he leave the force? But if he did, what would he do instead? It was all too much: his brain was too tired and his legs as shaky as Crane's. He was a mess.

"Come in, Derek," he heard Grimes shout as he approached the Chief Super's door.

Anderson sat down heavily on the chair his boss indicated, and forced his hands down onto his lap, instead of up to wipe his face. He waited for the criticism he was certain was coming.

"I hear you've found a film of the killing of one of our victims."

"Yes, sir, from a nanny cam the victim had in her bedroom."

"It's pretty horrible from the looks of you."

Anderson decided to be blunt. "It's the worst thing I've ever seen. I can't seem to process it, sir."

"You will, Derek, it will just take a bit of time that's all."

"Really?"

"Really. I witnessed a murder. Just the once, thank God." Grimes leaned back in his chair, the leather squeaking in protest. "We had this bloke holed up in a hostage situation. I offered to go in and talk to him, like the young fool I was. The room he was in smelled foul. Smelled of evil, you could say. A woman was lying on the floor, her chest covered in more blood than I'd ever seen. He'd shot her. In his arms he had a young girl. A gun was pressed to her temple. I put my hands up to show I was unharmed. I tried to talk him down. It didn't work. He shot the girl's brains out in front of me. Then turned the gun on himself."

Anderson wondered what he was supposed to say. He really couldn't think of anything suitable, so stayed silent.

"It was a week before I could keep any food down. It took me a long time to get over that, I can tell you. I very nearly left the force. Made my mind up to do it several times."

"But you didn't." Anderson finally found his voice.

"No. I reckoned what happened that day had to be

the worst I'd ever face. And as I'd already paid my dues, surely things could only get better, not worse."

"And did they?"

"Yes. Thank goodness. I never came across anything like that again. But what it did do was to make me even more determined to stop evil, where ever I found it. It takes an extraordinary man to be a good police officer, Derek. You're one of those men. I'd hate to lose you because of this."

Anderson wondered if it was obvious he was feeling beaten. His face and body must have given him away. Mind you he wasn't exactly trying to hide his emotions.

"Your team need you and your victims need you. Do it for them. Do it for the three souls whose lives he's taken. Make sure he pays the price for this depraved killing spree. Go home and spend the evening with the family. A good meal, a couple of drinks and a good night's sleep will help. Take it from someone who knows."

Anderson nodded. Not trusting himself to speak he simply stood and left the room. He still struggled under the weight of the case, as though buckling under the burden of the cross, dragging it along with him as it rested firmly on his shoulders. But Grimes had sown the seed of endurance. Anderson only hoped he could nurture that feeling, so it grew and flowered. He hoped his family could provide the sustenance it needed. With a new respect for the boss, he pushed out of the building and made his way to the comfort of home.

Theresa

Theresa and Tim had hardly spoken since the debacle a few days ago at the police station. She'd avoided him and he her. Tim was now spending even more hours at work, or wherever the hell it was that he was spending his time. She was dozing on the bed, something she seemed to be doing more frequently, unaware of the passage of time.

Tim had come home a couple of evenings after work, found the house cold and dark, with no meal ready and had turned and walked straight back out again. She'd heard him from the sanctuary of her bed. She couldn't blame Tim. But couldn't warm to him either. She didn't know how to get back to the place where she'd trusted him. Even if it turned out he wasn't that awful killer, as she and the police suspected he was, then why had he really been in Aldershot, Portsmouth and Southampton?

To her it still seemed extremely unlikely he was telling the truth when he said he was on university business. It had all combined to force a barrier between them. Life wasn't some *Star Trek* adventure where a ray gun could pierce an invisible force field. If it was, then her ray gun was clearly out of juice.

The phone rang on the bedside table. She nearly let it

ring out, but at the last minute picked it up and managed to mumble some sort of greeting into the receiver.

"Mrs Dennison?"

It was the Crane bloke from the police, she recognised his voice. "Yes, what is it?" She couldn't be bothered with social niceties.

He went on to explain they'd had a breakthrough in the murder cases. They were no longer looking at Tim. It wasn't him. It wasn't her. In fact the case had absolutely nothing to do with either of them.

"Nothing?"

"No, Mrs Dennison, nothing. So we won't be bothering you again."

She was sure that implicit in those words was the instruction that she wasn't to bother them again, either. She didn't want to talk to Crane anymore, so she replaced the receiver. But she fumbled in the dim room and the phone ended up crashing to the floor, the dialling tone wailing. She left it where it was.

She was stunned by Crane's words. The murders weren't anything to do with either of them. If that was the case, then what the hell had Tim been up to? The question pierced the dullness surrounding her. It was as if light had flooded into the bedroom and she could see clearly again.

Struggling upright, she swung her legs off the bed and staggered into the bathroom, her feet stiff and unfeeling after many hours of lying down. Turning the power shower on full, she shed the clothes she'd been wearing for the last three days. Shivering, she stepped into the shower and let the hot water cascade over her.

By the time Tim was due home, the house was in order. She'd let her standards slip over the past week, as she'd been spending more time in bed than out of it. She hadn't had a tin of polish or a duster in her hand for ages. The house felt unloved. Uncared for. A reflection of herself. But she was determined to change.

It was nearly 8pm by the time he walked through the front door. Being greeted by the smell of a rather good goulash and the sound of a nice bottle of red being uncorked, seemed to relax him. When he sat at the table she asked if he'd had a phone call from Crane as well and he nodded that he had, as he ate a forkful of food.

As she picked at her own meal, she wondered aloud if she needed psychiatric help, as she had become so obsessed with him being the killer.

"I'm sorry for not trusting you, Tim," she said. "It was a horrible thing I did, thinking you were a murderer and I'm ashamed I contacted Aldershot police. There must be something wrong with me. I don't know how I could treat my husband of twenty-five years that way."

She noticed Tim had gone rather pale and his hand was shaking as he reached for his wine glass.

"Tim? What's wrong?"

She had to endure his close scrutiny for a while before he spoke. "I think it's about time I con… told you what has been happening. It's not right that you're doubting your sanity. It's true, I was away on the nights of the murders, but I hope you now understand it was only a co-incidence."

"Of course I do, Tim, I've just told you that. What do you mean by 'it's about time you confessed'? That's what you were going to say wasn't it? What do you have to confess to?" Theresa became aware she was screwing her napkin up, twisting and turning it in clawed fingers and threw it down onto the table.

"I'm having an affair," he said, looking at the table instead of her. "But not with a woman."

Tears were threatening now and she fought against them, lifting her glass to her lips to take a reviving mouthful.

"With a man."

Suddenly Theresa seemed to be in a vacuum. All the air seemed to have been sucked out of the room. She forgot to breathe.

The glass slipped out of her hand. The bottom of it bounced on the table and gravity did the rest. She heard herself gasp for air and Tim choke as he tried to drink a glass of water. The clock ticked behind her and a car horn blared somewhere outside.

Theresa felt disassociated from reality, from her feelings. It was as if she were floating above the table, watching, as her life shattered into as many pieces as the glass on the floor.

"I think I better leave," he said. "I'll come along later in the week and collect some of my belongings. I really am sorry, Theresa. But it's for the best that it's out in the open. It's no reflection on you, honestly. It's me. All me."

She heard him move into the hall. His car keys rattled as he collected them from the dish and the fabric of his coat whispered as he shrugged into it. The sound of the door closing behind him was the softest of clicks. No slamming. No anger. No recriminations. No shouted arguments like in the romance novels she enjoyed.

The silence surrounding her felt wrong. So she shouted into it, screaming out the years of her marriage. She picked up Tim's wine glass and threw it against the wall. Jagged bits of glass and wine covered the floor and were soon joined by the new Habitat plates they'd been eating off. The Pyrex casserole dish containing the remains of the goulash proved harder to smash, but the contents of it sprayed satisfyingly around the walls.

The anger left her as quickly as it had arrived and she sank to the floor crying for her marriage, her ruined life and the wasted years, oblivious to her cut feet and hands, her blood mingling with the pools of red wine.

Holly

"Sorry, guv, that's the best I can do?"

"Really?" Anderson asked Holly.

"Honest. The only similar looking faces to our suspect are around Newcastle and Scotland, with one in the US and one in Australia. He's obviously been very careful and doesn't use his real photo on any social media."

"That's buggered us then," said Anderson, throwing his reading glasses onto his desk.

"So, I reckon it's back to my idea, sir."

"What?"

"Only this time if I arrange meetings at a local pub, we'll know if the bloke who turns up is the right one, because we know what he looks like. And he doesn't know that we know, if you get my drift."

To Holly it seemed to make perfect sense. She wouldn't be in danger and would be surrounded by coppers in the pub in plain clothes. "I don't see how else we can find him. We have to set up a sting and draw him out."

"I reckon you're right. Let me think on it and check with Grimes."

"Must we?" Holly could see her plan going down the drain again, along with her enthusiasm for the job. She could almost hear the death gurgles as it swirled around the plug hole.

"It's alright, Holly, I reckon we'll get a green light this time, but you know I can't miss out that step. Not if I want to keep my job. And you yours, by the way."

"Yes, guv."

"So, off you go and write up your plan and do a risk analysis…"

"Oh no, guv, me?"

Anderson put his glasses back on and looked at her over the top of them.

"Okay, okay, I'm on it."

Holly slunk back to her desk. She hated paperwork, forms to fill in, requests to be made, search warrants applied for. All she wanted to do was to immerse herself in her computer programmes, searching and probing and doing the stuff she was best at. Mind you, at least she'd get a chance to be at the sharp end of policing for a change, rather than holed up in the office. Get out into the sunshine. No, scrub that, step into the darkness of a smelly pub.

"You alright, Hols, are you talking to yourself?"

She looked up to find Ciaran grinning at her, his phone, as usual, glued to his hand. He took it everywhere with him now, scared to miss a call from Donna. That woman had him on a bloody string. Holly couldn't understand the attraction. Who wanted a painted doll, a glorified waitress in the air, all white teeth and hair spray? No, her tastes ran to a more natural look, although she preferred her girlfriends to be more feminine than she herself was. She supposed straight people would class her as 'the male' in a lesbian couple, but that was only something conjured up by those who liked to put peoples in boxes. And Holly wasn't a box kind of person.

"Yeah, cool thanks, just mulling something over. You?"

"Just waiting for Donna to call to say she's landed. We're going out for a meal tonight."

"Nice," she said and turned back to her computer to start outlining her plan.

Not being someone who waited for permission to put something into action, as soon as she'd realised there would be no luck with facial recognition on their killer, she'd put another profile up on S-Dates and had already had a couple of responses. So it was only a matter of agreeing a meeting, at a suitable place, with the two men who'd shown an interest in participating in the more adventurous kind of sex.

It was raining hard the night of the sting, which they hoped wouldn't put either of the two men they were waiting for, off. In the end Holly had only managed to get two of the men who had responded to her listing on S-Dates, to agree to meet. But two were better than none. She'd asked for photos, but neither man would send one, instead agreeing to meet towards the back of The Goose public house in Aldershot. The men would be wearing a trilby hat and her, well she would have on her ever present cargo pants and hoped each would find the other. Sitting where agreed and looking around, she saw no one was wearing a trilby á la Olly Murs, so she figured the first man still wasn't there.

Ciaran was at the bar, with Donna of all people. He'd said it was a chance meeting, but Holly hadn't believed a word of it. Ciaran had then said it would make his presence seem more natural, a bloke out with his bird for a drink. Holly thought Crane was going to throw him out of the pub when he'd found out, but Anderson had calmed him down, pointing out it would do no one any good if they created a scene. At the very least it would ruin the whole operation. So Ciaran had been allowed to stay, as had Donna, who'd said if anyone had a right to be there at the arrest, she had. After all it was her best friend who had been killed. Holly thought that rather over the top, bearing in mind the woman was hardly ever home and had known very little about her so called best friend. But for once she'd managed to keep her mouth shut. There had been little point in inflaming the situation, otherwise the whole thing would have been cancelled and who knew when she'd get another chance to be involved in an undercover operation. And, besides, she was having too much fun.

"You alright, Holly?" the voice in her ear made her jump. Bugger, she still hadn't got used to the communications system.

"Yes, thanks, Crane," she mumbled into her wrist, feeling a bit stupid.

"There's a bloke on his way in, complete with hat."

She nodded, then realised she should have spoken and quickly said, "Okay." She pulled out her mobile phone and played with it, so she would look like everyone else in the pub. "Does he look like our man?"

"Not sure, couldn't see him properly."

Before she could reply to Crane a man walked up to her. "Hey, Holly?"

They'd decided to use her real name as it was sufficiently different and there would be less room for confusion. There were just too many Emily's, Amber's and Jessica's around at the moment.

"John?" she asked, standing. At his nod of agreement she said, "You're not like I imagined you."

Upon hearing the code sentence, Ciaran and Crane appeared like Will-o'-the-wisps suddenly manifesting and each grabbed an arm.

"Oy, what the hell do you think you're doing?" John struggled against them as his fellow drinkers turned to look.

"Aldershot Police. Don't say anything, just turn round and calmly walk out of the pub with us. Got it?"

The menace was clear in Crane's voice and he'd turned little old John from belligerent to bewildered in an instant. She couldn't blame him. Crane would have scared the shit out of her too.

John dramatically nodded his head in agreement and did as they asked. Holly sat down with a thump on her seat, not realising how rigid she'd been with nerves until it was over. Donna was watching her, eyes wide with excitement. But Holly wasn't excited. John wasn't the one they were looking for. Maybe the next one wouldn't be either. What a disappointment that would turn out to be. But she had to remain positive, she berated herself.

The gawkers had gone back to their drinks as Holly asked, "All okay?" into her wrist.

"Fine, John has left. I don't think he'll be so quick to try and find a partner on the internet next time he's feeling randy though," said Crane, making Holly smile and feel better.

She went back to fiddling with her phone as Ciaran returned to the bar and took up his place with Donna, whose eyes were still as wide as saucers and she was looking at Ciaran with a new respect. So that's what this masquerade had been all about. The cunning fox. From the looks of her, Donna was practically eating out of

Ciaran's hand, smiling, laughing and touching his arm. Her adoration was clear. It looked like Ciaran had played a blinder.

Walking over to them at the bar, Holly ordered a sparkling water.

"You alright love?" the barman asked. "That was a strange stunt you lot pulled there."

"Yes, I'm fine thanks."

"So, what's going on?"

"Nothing," said Holly, but she wasn't able to meet his eye and shuffled the coins in her hand.

"Anything I should know about?"

"Um…"

"Just a spot of police business," Ciaran leaned over and flashed his badge.

"I gathered that," the barman said. "I just don't want my customers spooked and leaving in droves."

"They won't be. We'll be discreet."

"Fair enough. That one's on me, love," he said to her and turned away to serve someone else.

Ciaran grinned at Donna and puffed out his chest in importance, making Holly want to burst out laughing. But Donna was still in adoration mode and didn't seem to mind Ciaran's posturing.

Holly didn't have too much time to dwell on her colleague's love life, as this time Anderson's voice crackled in her ear.

"Look sharp, another one is on the way."

"Thanks, guv," Holly mumbled and returned to her seat once more looking at her phone. Although her head was slightly dipped towards the phone, she was looking over the top of it and noticed a straw hat with a black band around it bobbing over the heads of the other customers. The hat wove its way towards her and Holly steeled herself for another encounter.

The man who walked up to her, removed his hat and shook the water off it. "Good idea, the hat, considering the weather," he said and sat down in the chair opposite her without being asked. "I'm Darren," he said, "and you must be Holly. Want a drink?"

"I've already got one, thanks," she said. "Um, you're not like I imagined you to be."

"Really? Were you wanting a Greek God type? Sorry to disappoint, luv. Shall I leave now?"

"Yes," said Ciaran, who had moved up to stand behind Darren. "That would be a very good idea. Aldershot Police, now move."

Darren stumbled slightly as he rose and turned to look at Ciaran, the surprised look on his face worthy of any cartoon character and Holly had to laugh despite her disappointment. She gathered up her stuff and followed the two men out of The Goose. That was the end of that, she thought. Her deflation felt like a blown up balloon, released without knotting it, as it huffed and puffed its way around the room before falling to the floor. But a more sobering thought was - how else were they going to find their killer?

Boy

Naturally, I've always been interested in the psychoanalysis of those who practise BDSM in one form or another. It's a bit like, 'doctor, heal thyself', I suppose. Although the last thing I need is healing. The more I understand, the more I can come to terms with who I am and appreciate the needs of the others who I encounter from the BDSM community.

There are a number of reasons commonly given for why a sadomasochist finds the practise of S&M enjoyable, and apparently the answer is largely dependent on the individual – no shit Sherlock.

For some, taking on a role of compliance or helplessness offers a form of therapeutic escape from the stresses of life, from responsibility, or from guilt.

For others, being under the power of a strong, controlling presence may evoke the feelings of safety and protection associated with childhood. They likewise may derive satisfaction from earning the approval of that figure. That's me, don't you think?

But I'm changing as well. Perhaps I'm becoming more of a sadist. Sadists, it's said, may enjoy the feeling of power and authority that comes from playing the dominant role, or receive pleasure vicariously through the suffering of the masochist. Now I can relate to that one. Thanks to Sally for bringing that side of me out! And some psychologist or other said a sadomasochistic relationship, as long as it is consensual, is not a psychological problem. So it's official – I'm not mental, I'm just me.

The other thing I was right about is BDSM can have addiction-like tendencies, with several features resembling those of drug addiction: craving, intoxication, tolerance and withdrawal. No wonder I can't stop. Talking about Sally, she was the best. Numero Uno. Give that girl a gold medal. The others were good, but more of a silver and bronze medal if I'm honest. I'm still searching for another Sally. Someone who will take me to the heights of pleasure I've not reached since. I know it will happen.

That's what I crave.

The next high.

The next hit.

The next partner.

That's it. I can't believe I've been so stupid. There's only one place where I could even hope to feel how I felt that first time. It's so simple, I wonder why I didn't realise it before.

All I need to do is to recreate my encounter with Sally.

Donna

Donna was in the middle of tidying the flat, when a knock at the door made her jump. Still not entirely comfortable with being back at home, what with Sally's murder and all, she had taken to cleaning over and over again. Almost as if she were scrubbing away any trace of the vile monster who had killed Sally. And she wasn't using bleach. Even the faintest whiff of the stuff made her nauseous now. Glancing at her watch she wondered who it could be. Wishing she'd installed the spy hole Ciaran had told her to put into the door, she opened it slightly.

"Hi, is Sally in?"

Stood before her was a very personable young man, in his mid-twenties probably. He was asking about Sally? Donna hesitated.

"I've been working overseas," he said. "I lost my mobile phone, so haven't been able to keep in touch. I told her I'd ring when I got back and we'd go out. Dinner or something."

This was the stuff of nightmares. How could she tell him Sally had died? "Um, hi, I'm her flat mate, Donna."

"Can I come in?"

He began to walk through the door into the flat without giving her a chance to say no. But surely it would be alright? If he was a friend of Sally's.

Closing the door behind him, she turned and said, "I'm so sorry, I don't know how to tell you this… but…"

"What?"

"Sally's dead," she blurted, all her training as an air hostess flying out of the window. So much for being discreet and professional.

He sat down abruptly on the sofa. Donna wasn't entirely happy with that either, but she couldn't exactly grab hold of him and pull him up.

"Have I seen you before?" she asked him. "I'm sure you look familiar."

"That's probably because Sally and I had been seeing each other on and off, you know."

"No, I didn't know that. She never said."

"Well, it was more of an 'off' than an 'on' thing, you know? Christ, I can't believe she's dead. What happened? Was it an accident?"

"No, she was …"

That was it! That's where she'd seen his face, from the sting at the Goose the other night. It was the man from the photo. "… murdered." She managed to finish her sentence and made a grab for her mobile.

"Waiting for a call from someone?" he said, and Donna was sure she heard a slightly sinister edge to his voice.

"Yes, my boyfriend. He must have been delayed. I'm just checking to see if he's sent a message." Turning her back on her intruder, she called Ciaran's number, then turned down the volume, turned off the screen and kept it in her hand.

"It's funny Sally never mentioned you," she said. She

wanted to keep him talking, to give Ciaran a chance to understand what was going on. He would understand. She was sure of it. Yes, definitely he would.

"Well, you're away so often, maybe I was around when you weren't?"

"Maybe. I wonder where Ciaran is?" she said, looking at her watch. "He's normally so reliable. I can't believe he hasn't come over." She really wanted to shout that bit for Ciaran's benefit, but daren't antagonise the man in front of her. "He's in the police, you know?"

"Oh. Local plod is he?" he said, the veiled sneer not lost on Donna.

"No, major crimes actually. He's a really interesting person. I'm sure you'd get on. He's a very friendly bloke. What did you say your name was again?"

"I didn't. So is this where it happened?" he looked around the small living room.

"Where what happened?"

"Where Sally was killed?"

"Um, it was in her bedroom."

"Show me."

"What?" Donna's head jerked up from where she'd been looking at her phone again, not daring to turn the screen on in case he saw her phone was connected to Ciaran's.

"I said show me."

He grabbed at her arm and pushed her through the bedroom door in front of him.

"Let go of me," she shouted, "you're hurting me."

"I'll hurt you even more if you don't shut up."

By now, Ciaran was flying down the stairs in Aldershot Police Station. He'd put out a call for an emergency response team to Donna's address and was thanking all sorts of gods that, firstly she was only a few minutes' drive away from the police station, and secondly that she'd had the initiative to call him. Throwing open the door of his car, he started the engine and pulled away before he'd even closed it behind him.

He couldn't believe what was happening. Had he put her in danger by going out with her? But then again how could that be? Wild thoughts raced through his mind as he sped through the streets. He wondered if the Choker, for that's who it had to be, was armed. But no that was stupid. Aldershot wasn't the USA where every man and his dog had a gun. The Choker hadn't used a weapon before, as far as they were aware. But this time it was different. Donna wasn't a willing participant.

Ciaran wondered why the Choker had decided to go back to the scene of his first crime. Needing to recreate it perhaps? With Donna as a substitute for Sally? He moaned out loud and pressed down hard on the accelerator, with no thought for his own safety.

Donna's arms had just been tied to the bed when she heard them. Sirens. It seemed Ciaran had understood what was happening to her. She'd known she could depend on him but, if she was honest, her faith had wavered for a while there. She'd never been so frightened in all her life. It had all happened so fast. He'd pushed her into Sally's room and as she'd stumbled, he'd grabbed her hair and dragged her onto the bed. She put up her arms to try and free her hair and that's when he'd managed to hold onto first one and then the other of her wrists. He had pinned her body to the bed by kneeling on her chest, which had pushed all the air out of her lungs, so she was more interested in trying to breathe than with what he was doing to her arms. Now she was immobile. Struggle as she might, she couldn't free her hands.

Twisting her head to look up, she saw they were tied with plastic ties. Still looming over her, her attacker pulled a silk scarf out of his coat pocket. There was no doubt now, she was dealing with the Choker. He'd been pulling off her clothes when they heard the sirens. His head came up as he listened and realised what was happening.

"You bitch," he snarled and punched her in the face. Everything went black in an instant.

When she came round, confused and disorientated, Ciaran was bending over her.

"Donna, are you alright? Say something for God's sake!"

"Ciaran?" she mumbled through lips that were swelling and splitting. She tasted blood on her tongue.

"It's all over. He's gone," Ciaran said. "I was so frightened," he whispered in her ear.

"So was I!" She tried to grin, but her lip split even more and she had to stop.

"Try not to talk," he said. "The bastard punched you in the face. We're going to get you to hospital and have you checked over. Did he do anything else to you?"

She shook her head, then realised she was cold and shaking. Her jeans had gone and she was dressed only in her knickers and ripped tee-shirt. Ciaran tenderly untied each wrist and then put her hands in plastic bags before gently helping her bring her arms down to her side, as she couldn't feel them. She groaned as the pins and needles started as the blood began to flow again.

"Can you give us some room, sir," a deep voice said behind Ciaran.

"Yes, sorry," she heard Ciaran say. Then his head bent to hers again. "It's just the paramedics, they're going to take you to hospital. But you need to keep the plastic bags on your hands, until we can get samples from under your nails. There might be some skin cells under there."

"Alright, but don't leave me," she begged as her resolve to be brave dissolved and the tears came.

"No chance. I'll be right by your side."

Crane

Derek, Crane and Holly were lounging in Derek's office, looking at the photo of The Choker pinned up on the whiteboard and brainstorming what to do next. They were all still shocked from the events of the previous evening and were waiting for Ciaran to return with some decent coffee from a local specialist coffee shop, something Crane was looking forward to drinking. He knew it was a luxury and pricey, but had decided it was worth it. A decent shot of caffeine really helped him feel better, more alert and less in a fog with the pain. Okay so he was swapping one drug for another, but at least caffeine wasn't so addictive. Or at least he hoped not.

Ciaran hadn't wanted to come to work, desperate to stay by Donna's side, but she'd told him not to be so stupid and to pull himself together, so he could find the bastard who'd hurt her and killed Sally. When he'd appeared in the office he was a physical and emotional wreck, which is why Crane had sent him out for the coffees.

Everyone in the team had been badly shaken by the Choker re-appearing at Sally's apartment. But he'd got away again. The sirens had alerted him and whilst it had stopped him killing Donna, it had meant she'd been badly beaten for her treachery, before he'd slipped away into the night. Officers were going through local CCTV cameras but Crane didn't hold out much hope. CCTV worked really well during the day, but at night? Not such good results.

His introspection was broken by Derek asking, "What do you think, Crane?"

"Think? Sorry, you'll have to repeat that."

Derek huffed theatrically then said, "What do you think about releasing the photo of the killer to the media? I think we're out of ideas to be honest. Going public is the only option left to us."

"If he sees it, it will alert him to the fact that we know what he looks like, but not who he is. He could change his look because of it."

"Change his look?"

"Yeah, different hair colour, grow a beard, moustache, that sort of thing."

"Oh, I get you," Holly said. "But surely if someone who knows him sees it, then they'll respond to the request for help, won't they?"

"What about publishing it in the form of an e-fit?" said Derek.

"An e-fit of who?" said Ciaran walking into the room and interrupting the discussion while they each grabbed their coffee from him and Holly picked up her green tea.

"Our killer," said Crane after a satisfying sip. "Rather than use his photo from the nanny cam, doctor it so it looks like an e-fit."

"What's the point of that?"

"So we can say it was an e-fit of a person described by a victim who survived."

"But it wouldn't be," said Holly.

"But he wouldn't know," said Ciaran.

"That's lying," she insisted.

"That's police work," laughed Anderson. "That's a great idea, Crane. Let's see if we can't rattle his cage a bit, make him worry, that's when offenders tend to make mistakes."

"But he's been very clever so far," said Holly.

"Who has?"

Everyone turned to look at the speaker. It was Professor Dennison.

"Him?" he asked as he stared at the photograph. "It can't be."

"Professor, are you alright?" Crane reached out to hold the man's elbow, but as that made the two of them unstable, Ciaran came to his aid and pushed a chair behind Dennison's knees just as his legs gave way. He sat down with a small puff of air from the cushioned seat.

Crane grabbed the back of the Professor's chair with one hand and his stick with the other and just about managed to stay upright. "Why are you here?" he blurted.

"I, um, came to apologise and to explain where I was on the nights of the murders. One of your colleagues showed me up. I felt it was the least I could do. A kind of penance because you'd wasted so much time investigating me. But now I've seen this… who is it?"

"Our murderer."

"Are you sure?" Dennison's voice was high and reedy, like an old man trying and failing to be assertive.

"We're sure," said Derek. "Why? Do you recognise him?"

"I'm very much afraid I do," said Dennison, causing Crane to wobble and sit down on the nearest chair. Bugger standing up. He'd had a shock. They'd all had a shock.

"How?"

"Why?"

"Who is he?"

"Bloody hell."

They all spoke at once.

Crane took several deep breaths and then a healthy slug of coffee to revive him.

Anderson

"He's one of my students."

"Jesus."

"Who'd have thought?"

"Christ."

"If you've all finished," Anderson decided to take control of his team. "Professor, can you explain, please. Tell us everything you know about him."

After a deep breath he spoke. "He's one of my students."

"Studying criminology?"

"Yes. He's also in my tutor group."

"So you know him well?" Anderson felt a bubble of excitement rising up through his chest. Although it could be trapped wind. His stomach was constantly clenched with stress these days, what with all the murders and Crane fucking about with those little pills of his, not to mention Ciaran mooning over someone connected to the case, and Holly turning out to be a regular Miss Marple. Anderson struggled to concentrate. The Professor's revelation that he knew their killer had come so suddenly, he was having trouble focusing his thoughts. He felt like all the air had been forced out of his lungs, and for a moment was as unsteady on his feet as Crane usually was. He decided to stop fighting the feeling of vertigo and sat down himself.

"What's his name?" Derek asked the Professor.

"Giles Acreman."

"We need to know everything about him."

The Professor nodded. "The best bet is his student file."

"Can you get me a copy?" Anderson, at last, was absorbing the shock and beginning to think more like a policeman and less like a drunk.

"If I can go and get my laptop from the car, I can remotely log into the university intranet and access his records for you."

"That's great," said Holly. "I can copy the files and then print them out."

Professor Dennison stood and Anderson noticed he was still very unstable. He suddenly looked much older than in his late forties. He seemed to have aged ten years since walking in the door only ten minutes ago. "Ciaran will go with you," Anderson said, "and carry your case."

The young DC sprung up. "This way, Professor. Would you like a coffee when we get back?"

Satisfied that Profession Dennison was in good hands, Derek turned to Holly. "Get everything we've got on this Giles Acreman while we're waiting."

"Yes, guv, although it might not be much. I'll try social media as well, but as the facial recognition didn't work…" Holly said and left the room.

"Well I'll be buggered," he turned to Crane.

"Who'd have thought it would be that easy. It almost feels like a let-down."

"That's police work for you. But don't be complacent. We haven't got him in custody yet. Nor have we any evidence he killed Charlie and Dawn. Remember we only have him on the nanny cam killing Sally."

"Don't forget that Donna can bring a complaint against him for attempted rape. I'm not letting him get away with that. So, what's the plan for arresting him?"

"That's what we've got to work out. I've a few more questions for the Professor first and depending on that, we'll work out a plan."

Half an hour later they were organised. The Professor had had a restorative cup of tea, Holly had printed out the file, and they were all in Anderson's office. Holly took the lead, at the request of Anderson, who figured Dennison still wasn't at all steady on his feet, despite claims to the contrary. Anderson could feel they were coming to the end of the investigation. The danger was the team would relax. Be so thankful they knew who their killer was, they wouldn't see the arrest of him as being a problem. Anderson hoped they wouldn't encounter any difficulties, but you never knew.

"Giles Acreman," Holly was saying. "Student at Reading University, studying Criminology, which is a bit ironic to say the least."

"Stick to the facts please, Holly."

"Sorry, guv. Aged twenty-one, three years into a four year Honours Degree. Lives in a shared student house in Earley, giving him easy access to the university. Grades are good, looking at a 2.1 if his dissertation is good enough next year. We have his mobile phone number. I'm guessing he doesn't have a car as he's never applied for a parking permit. Parents both dead, his mother fifteen years ago, his father recently. No other family that I've been able to trace."

"Does he have a record?"

"He'd been reported to the university authorities once

for stalking, but has no police record at all, not even a warning or a caution." Having finished, Holly sat down at the table with the others.

"Stalking, eh?" said Crane. "That's a good place to start. Shows he's an obsessive personality."

"What do you make of him, Professor?" Anderson was keen to have a personal perspective.

"Good student, always does his assignments, hands them in on time, gets good grades for them. If anything he's a bit too quiet during tutor groups. Rather than joining in a discussion, he tends to sit there with a smirk on his face. As if he's better than all of us, you know? It gives me the creeps sometimes. But I always saw it as a minor point. It was just his personality. I didn't realise it was hiding something far darker. It looks like we were both concealing a darker side of ourselves."

As the Professor pulled out a handkerchief and wiped his eyes, Anderson said, "Professor Dennison, none of this is your fault. Do you understand?"

The Prof nodded his head and tried a watery smile, but he was clearly not convinced. He'd explained to Crane and Anderson in private, while they were waiting for Holly and Ciaran to complete the background checks, that the reason he'd been in the area on the nights of the three murders was because he was a closet gay and had been having liaisons, as he'd put it. He'd told them he'd confessed his secret to Theresa. Of course their marriage was now over and he was currently sleeping in his room at the university.

"I doubt she'll ever want to see me again," he'd said. "All communication is being done via our sons. I've hurt her very badly, I know. But I just can't help myself. I am what I am and it's about time I took responsibility for that. For years I pushed my sexual leanings deep down inside of me. In the end the secret was eating me from the inside out. I had to find out who I really was. I made contact with other men through S-Dates. I was petrified to start with, but with each encounter I became more comfortable with my sexual leanings and learned being gay wasn't the life sentence I'd imagined it to be. I needed to be good to myself, embrace who I was and enjoy it. Unfortunately Theresa has paid the price for my sexual freedom. I hope one day she'll realise I can't help being who I really am, not who I was pretending to be."

Anderson had felt sorry for the man, who was carrying two burdens. The first, the wilful destruction of his marriage and the second, his failing to see that one of his students was a murderer, a serial killer. But there was no place for emotion now, all their focus had to been on apprehending Giles Acreman.

"When do you see him next?" Anderson asked.

Fumbling through his diary, Prof Dennison said, "Oh my God. Tomorrow!" The diary fell out of his trembling hands and Ciaran bent to pick it up.

"What's the occasion?" Crane asked.

"A lecture, in Foxhill House, where the School of Law is situated."

"Does he usually attend them?"

"Oh yes, I've never known him miss one. He's obsessive. I don't think he's missed anything in the past three years."

"That's all very well," mused Crane. "But we can't bank on him being there, Derek."

"No, I agree. I think we put teams on the lecture hall and also on his house. If he's not at one, he should be at the other."

"But there are lots of spots in the university grounds where he could slip out of the campus. You know in case he sees us and gets away." Holly said, then went back to chewing the top of her pen.

"How about police cars at those points? I'm sure Reading would be glad to help."

"Stop with the sarcasm, Crane," said Anderson. "I'll make sure they are."

The major crimes teams were still having problems liaising with some local police forces, who perceived them as undermining their own work and casting doubt on their ability to do their job. Sometimes it was jealously, sometimes resentment. Whichever, it was a bloody nuisance as far as Anderson and his team were concerned.

"What time is the lecture, Professor?"

Once they had all the details, Anderson said, "We've only got twenty-four hours, so I need your best work, people. Professor could you go with Holly please and work on the logistics of the site? Ciaran contact Reading Police and get the name and details of a Senior Officer who can lead the team from their end. Crane, write the Risk Analysis, incorporating all the information from Ciaran and Holly. I'm off to see Grimes and tell him the good news. Come on then, why are you all still sitting here? Off you go and make it happen."

Crane

"With attractive views of Whiteknights Lake and surrounded by parkland, the School of Law is situated in an architecturally significant Grade 2 listed building on the university's main campus."

Crane put the brochure down and instead of looking at the photographs in it, looked out of the car window at the building he'd been reading about. Foxhill House was grand and imposing, built in a Gothic revival style. The diamond pattern on the walls caught the eye immediately, giving the brickwork a texture that plain brick couldn't. Three stories high, the attic windows all had peaked arches above them, and at either end of the building were large chimney stacks, each one comprising three chimney pots.

He carried on reading aloud, "The house was originally built in 1868 by the architect Alfred Waterhouse and used as his own residence until he built an even more ambitious house, Yattendon Court. After that, a string of local dignitaries had owned it, before it was incorporated into Reading University.

"Foxhill was described in an auctioneer's advertisement in 1890 as a moderately sized gothic mansion with first class stabling, a coachman's and gardener's cottages and a small farm. The exterior of Foxhill has altered very little over the years. In the 2003 refurbishment, three new offices were added, linking the main house to the stable block, and the conservatory was replaced to provide two large teaching rooms with picture windows. Sadly, the Turkish baths in the basement no longer exist but many of the original features remain."

The building was certainly out of the way of the rest of the university buildings, the large site having grassland to the front and large wooded areas and the lake at the rear. All in all, a tranquil site, ideal for a seat of learning, if you liked that sort of thing, he supposed. It was a bloody nightmare for the police.

The nearest buildings were several halls of residence, the main campus being some way away. Once the lecture was underway, the three vehicular accesses into Reading University would have teams of police at them, checking the identity of those entering and leaving the site. The nearest pedestrian access points were on Upper Redlands Road and at the corner with that and Whiteknights Road, both of which would be covered. Police dog handlers would patrol the wood and lake area behind Foxhill House. The idea was to not frighten Acreman off, but to make like it was a normal day as he arrived. The police presence would only appear once the lecture started, by which time they hoped their prey would be safely inside Foxhill House.

Crane and Anderson were sitting in an unobtrusively placed car and had spent the last fifteen minutes watching students arriving for Professor Dennison's lecture. The last of the stragglers had just sprinted their way to the building. They had been really hoping to see

Giles Acreman walking into Foxhill House, but had had no such luck. And anyway, everyone seemed to look the same: jeans, trainers and hoodies. Didn't the young have any imagination when it came to attire, Crane wondered?

"Ready, Crane?" asked Anderson.

"As I'll ever be," he replied and climbed out of the car.

Tim

Professor Dennison was standing in the wings. His gown hung heavy on his shoulders and seemed too much of a weight for him to bear. He was physically and mentally exhausted.

After everything that had happened over the past few weeks, he was finding it difficult to function normally. His brain was sluggish, his arms felt like lead and his legs like jelly.

He didn't know where Anderson and his team were. The DI had felt it best he didn't, otherwise he may spend much of his time looking at them and therefore might give away their location. And the students might wonder who the newbies were. Particularly Acreman.

A shudder passed through him at the thought of the depraved things his student was capable of. How easily he'd been hoodwinked by the charming smile and air of confidence he'd always put down to Acreman being knowledgeable on the subject matter in hand, because of good preparation and planning.

But now it seemed it hid something other than that - something dark and evil.

He looked at his watch. He was already five minutes

late starting. He better get on with the lecture. He took one shaky step forward. Then another. He felt like a robot taking its first steps after being re-programmed.

Holly

Holly and Ciaran were standing at the top of the lecture hall looking down on the body of students. They had been chosen to sit in the hall as they were the only ones who wouldn't look out of place. Holly wore her normal cargo pants and a muddy coloured top and Ciaran had ditched his shirt and tie for a tee-shirt extolling a local rock band, and his leather shoes for trainers.

Ciaran poked Holly with his elbow. About to berate him for it, she looked at his face. Excitement seemed to be the overriding expression, but she noticed his eyes were wide with fear.

"Five rows down," he said. "Towards your side."

Holly craned her neck, but couldn't see Acreman. Deciding she'd just have to trust Ciaran, she nodded and walked to the stairs to her left. Ciaran walked to those to his right. Stepping down towards Acreman's row, Holly was surprised to find her legs were as useless as a new born lamb's and she stumbled. She would have fallen down the steps if she hadn't been caught by someone.

"Hey," a voice said. "You alright?"

"Fine thanks."

Her knight in shining armour was bending over her.

He was so close, the smell of his aftershave filled her nostrils. She shrugged off his hand and stood up, holding onto the back of the first seat in the row nearest to her.

"Here, sit down next to me," the man said, "before you tumble all the way down and knock the Prof over."

Sinking into the seat at the end of the row Holly looked up to see who the owner of the voice was. Even though she wasn't remotely interested in men, she had to admit his dulcet tones were like chocolate, coating her in its sugary sweetness. Expecting a six pack, muscled poster boy, the face floating in front of her was the stuff of nightmares. She was staring at Giles Acreman.

"I'm Giles," he said grinning.

"Holly."

"Not seen you here before."

Christ. Stunned, she realised she was going to have to make polite conversation. Not a forte of hers. "No, I've just switched over," she mumbled.

"From?"

Bloody hell, she thought. Switched from… "Sociology," she managed. "Decided being a social worker wasn't quite for me."

"Wouldn't be for me either," he smiled. "Hope this is a better fit. Dennison's quite good. I think you'll like him."

Luckily, the Professor chose that moment to walk onto the stage, saving her from further conversation. Her left leg was shaking with involuntary tremors, so she crossed her legs in the cramped space, hoping that by putting her good leg on top of the shaking one, it would stop.

"You okay?" he hissed.

"Yeah, must have hurt my leg. I'll be fine."

"Do you need paper?"

"What?"

He held up a notebook. Christ, this was getting worse and worse. "No, I've got one here. Thanks anyway."

She put her hand in the pocket on her left leg and fumbled to get out her small notebook and pen. Jesus. She was having a hot flush and began to fan her face with her pad. She wasn't trained for this. Her mind was screaming for Ciaran to come and help her. Turning in her seat, she caught a glimpse of Crane and Anderson walking into the back of the hall, giving her an idea.

Tim

"So, today, we're going to look at… look at…" Dennison realised that he'd forgotten to click the button to change the slide.

"Sorry, to take a look at theories of crime – sociological and theoretical accounts of offending."

He had never felt less like talking to a body of students. It reminded him of when he'd first started lecturing, the panic and sense of overwhelming fear that he wasn't good enough, didn't know enough. Who was he to educate young, hungry minds? He was back there now, fuelled by the lack of self-worth he was currently feeling. All he'd managed to do lately was upset people.

Pressing the button, he said, "We're here to try and identify and explain a range of theoretical approaches to issues concerning crime as a phenomenon, offenders and offending, and social responses to crime."

Looking up he could see the majority of the students were scribbling, some tapping at phones and tablets and others watching him closely. One of those staring at him was Giles Acreman.

Dennison managed to press the button. "Um, crime as, a, um, ah, phenom… phenom…"

"Phenomenon!" someone shouted, startling him and bringing him back from his bleak thoughts about Acreman.

"Thank you, young sir," he managed a mock bow. "Perhaps you'd be so kind as to give us your thoughts on the subject." That, thankfully, took the spotlight off him, giving him a couple of minutes to catch his breath.

He managed to continue with his lecture for a further few minutes, until movement at the end of one of the rows caused him to stutter again. If he wasn't mistaken, Holly and Giles Acreman were making their way up the stairs towards the exit at the back of the hall.

Holly

"Oh God," Holly said, swaying in her seat, "I don't feel too good."

Acreman looked at her and must have agreed with her as he said, "Quick, put your head between your legs."

She managed to uncross them, then felt Giles' hand on the back of her head, insistently pushing it forward. She allowed him to do so, swallowing down her panic at his touch but she couldn't stop the shaking it produced.

He said, "Perhaps you need some fresh air?"

Holly managed to nod and slid off her seat. She tried to move into the aisle, but her legs started to fold in on themselves. They were no longer able to hold her weight. Acreman grabbed hold of her arm and pulled her upright.

"Come on, I'll help you. Up you go."

By now Holly was no longer faking it. She only just managed to put one foot in front of the other, aiming for where she'd last seen Anderson and Crane standing. Please God, she prayed, let them still be there.

Ciaran

Ciaran had seen the commotion at the other end of the row. Bugger, was Holly alright? His first instinct was to push along the row to get to her. But he realised that would be a very bad move indeed. Either she was making a play, or there was really something wrong with her. He very much hoped it was the former. He'd never forgive himself if something happened to her. She was really brave, he knew, always coming up with ideas about how to catch the Choker, but he also knew she had limited experience of police work. She was a civilian analyst after all.

Holly was being helped up the steps by Acreman, who seemed to be supporting her, as they climbed upward. He stood up as quietly as he could, holding the seat so it wouldn't bang against the back and started mounting the stairs on his side, never taking his eyes from Holly. Which was a mistake. Acreman must have felt his scrutiny, for he looked over at Ciaran. Pausing, he then looked upward and must have seen Crane and Anderson who were waiting to grab Holly and Acreman as they reached the top of the stairs.

Acreman put on a spurt and pushed Holly in front of

him, thrusting her at Crane and Anderson, so they were unable to chase after him. Holly bumped against them, and down they went, all legs and arms and Crane's stick.

Ciaran matched Acreman's speed and was only a few strides behind him as he burst through the door… into the waiting arms of two of Reading's finest.

Crane

Giles Acreman was denying everything, along with a few well chosen, 'no comments'. He'd accepted the offer of a duty solicitor and the young woman had sat next to her client, with alternating expressions of shock and horror on her face, as they'd confronted him with the murder of three people and the attempted rape of one other.

Finally, with no viable alternative strategy, Anderson had taken the decision to tell him they had a video of him killing Sally Saunders.

Crane tapped the tablet he'd brought in with him to their third interview of Acreman. "It's on here," he said.

"How? Where from?" Acreman gabbled.

"Sally had a nanny cam, hidden in a smiley face on the wall in her bedroom."

By the change in Acreman's expression, Crane realised they had the right man. His desperation to see the video was disgusting to watch. Acreman looked like the big bad wolf from the fairy tale, licking his lips in anticipation, as he prepared to eat his prey.

"If you admit to the killings we'll let you see it," said Anderson, which of course was an outright lie, but Acreman didn't know that.

"How can I trust you? Maybe you're lying to get me to confess?"

"No, unfortunately I'm not," Crane went pale at the memory of the disgusting images that he still couldn't get out of his head and were giving him nightmares.

"Show me a bit now then," a sly smile crossed Acreman's face.

"Sorry?"

"Show me a bit now. Then I'll believe you and tell you everything."

Crane and Anderson look at each other. They'd anticipated this and had decided that their determination to get the creep to confess would make them do as he asked.

"Very well," said Crane.

Turning on the tablet, Crane showed Acreman the beginning of the video. The small screen of the tablet showed him and Sally entering her bedroom and moving towards the bed, before Crane abruptly turned it off.

"Oh my God, you really do have it!"

The salacious grin on Acreman's face made Crane want to throw up.

"We told you we did," said Anderson. "We weren't lying."

"Okay, okay so I did it."

"Did what?"

Crane was relieved Derek had taken over the interview as he doubted he could have spoken another word to the disgusting, depraved man sat in front of him.

"Killed them. The three of them." Acreman boasted.

"What are their names?"

"I don't know," he snorted. "I only knew their user names."

Crane knew that was an outright lie, as the

newspapers and television had named each victim.

"In that case, please identify them from theses photographs." Anderson opened a file and removed three photographs. "Here's the first, Sally Smith."

"Yeah, she was the first. Bloody exciting that was."

"Where did you meet her?"

"We arranged through S-Dates to meet at her flat. Her flatmate, Donna, was away so we had the place to ourselves. A lovely looking girl she was."

"Where was the flat?"

"Somewhere in Aldershot. I can't remember the address."

Crane's fists clenched at the audacity of the man. He might as well be saying 'no comment'. If he was trying to rile them, the tactic was definitely working on Crane.

"And that's where you recently returned to."

"Oh, right, poor Donna got her face bashed in didn't she? All her own fault, of course. She shouldn't have called that boyfriend of hers."

Anderson closed his eyes. Crane decided to give his friend a break and said, "Okay, what about the second?"

"The second? Let me see. Oh, yes, that was a bloke wasn't it? He was good looking as well, but then most of the gay men are. We met in Portsmouth. He had a place over a row of shops if I remember correctly."

"And the third?"

"The girl from Southampton. She wasn't as good as the others."

"Do you own a car?" Anderson asked.

"No, I went by train to all three. I've got my train stubs. I wanted to make a collection. A little shrine you might say, to them. They gave their lives so I could have the most orgasmic sex. It was only fitting that I revered them. I still think about them. Relive the experiences…."

Crane cut him short, unable to listen to any more of this revolting rambling. "I'm sure what you're telling us is the truth. We're going through your room now, so if the evidence that you say is there, we'll find it. You can count on that. There'll be CCTV coverage at the train stations as well. How did you get to the victims' homes from the railway stations?"

"I took taxis there, then ran most of the way back and caught the earliest train there was the next morning, back to Reading."

"We can corroborate that as well with the taxi companies. Well, I think that's about it." Crane looked to Anderson for his agreement.

"Thank you for your co-operation," Derek said and started to rise.

"What about the video?"

"An officer will come now and take your statement. We'll meet again after that."

"Make sure you do," Acreman said. "I'm not going anywhere. I'll still be here. See you with your laptop!" he shouted as they closed the door on him.

"I think that was the worst suspect interview I've ever done," said Anderson.

"But it looks like it will work. He's started talking already."

Crane turned to look through the one way mirror at their suspect. Anderson was right, Acreman couldn't wait to get his confession out and Ciaran was struggling to keep up with the words spilling from him, needing to try to keep the statement in some sort of coherent, logical order, for transcribing from the tape once they'd finished. Acreman's tongue kept wetting his lips. Crane was disgusted by the man's eagerness to boast about his activities.

Of course Acreman would never see the video. Once they had his statement, he'd be shunted back down to the cells and then after a brief appearance in Aldershot Magistrates Court, be sent off to prison to await his trial. They weren't sure who would represent him. As the three of them had left the interview room, the duty solicitor had promptly resigned. The poor girl looked traumatised and had said it didn't matter if she lost her job for her refusal. Anything was better than representing that creep.

"I'll send someone in with a mug of tea, just to sweeten the deal," said Anderson as they left the interview suite ready to go back upstairs to their office.

"Ha ha. Sorry but I seem to have left my sense of humour at home."

"Talking of home, how's Tina?"

"Bloody hell, she's become the Sargeant Major I used to be!"

"Really?" grinned Anderson.

"Really. Her and Major Martin have me very definitely under their thumbs. Talk about regimented. She watches me like a hawk to make sure I'm taking the tablets they dole out for me, and practically goes through my pockets every morning to make sure I've not slipped any extra tablets into my trousers or jacket."

Derek laughed at the image.

"You might laugh, but it's not funny to me, you know."

"But you're feeling better?"

Crane had to grudgingly admit he was. "The pain is under control now. I just get some increased discomfort when the tablets are running out. About an hour before the next dose is due I'd say. The Major has changed the

Tramadol to slow release, so they give a constant supply of pain killer, rather than a boost every 8 hours. It seems to have done the trick.

"And physiotherapy?"

Crane groaned. "I start again next week, now this case is just about sewn up. Three times a week, towards the end of the working day, so it shouldn't impact my job here too much."

By now they'd arrived outside the building, so Crane could have a cigarette.

"Where's your electronic one?" Anderson asked.

"That's another thing I need to get a handle on. Jesus, the list is bloody endless. Anyway, that's enough of my moaning, what about you?"

"Me?"

"Yes, Derek. You've taken this case really hard, haven't you?"

"Yes."

"Do you feel any better now we've got him?"

"Vaguely. I will when we have his signature on the bottom of a statement."

"And then?"

"Then we need an analysis of what went wrong with this case. How the hell we missed him at the three railway stations. Why we never canvassed taxi companies. How forensics missed that bloody nanny cam. Why did we have to rely on a stroke of luck to catch him?"

"That wasn't what I meant."

"I know, but that's all you're getting for now.

"Peter Sutcliffe was caught by a stroke of luck, when he was pulled over for a traffic misdemeanour. It doesn't mean our investigation was flawed. We would have got there eventually, you know."

"You're not helping, Crane. I'd be obliged if you'd

keep your opinions to yourself."

Crane stayed outside and watched his friend and colleague walk back into the station. His shoulders were still hunched, but Crane was sure he detected a little more spring in Anderson's step. At least he hoped so. He didn't think he could continue working without Derek at the helm of their little ship and he wondered how long it would take his friend to make the decision as to whether to continue in the job or not. He knew all about it, thanks to Tina talking to Derek's wife. But that was their little secret. In the meantime he'd just have to give Derek the space he needed to come to a decision.

He guessed the future would become clear, in time, not just for him and Derek, but for all of them. Donna was moving in with Ciaran and their relationship seemed to have been strengthened by Donna's experiences, rather than broken by it. And Holly? Well she had promised she'd spend the next case firmly anchored to her computers. Crane could only hope she'd get the chance to be as good as her word.

The End

Meet the Author

I do hope you've enjoyed Death Elements. If so, perhaps you would be kind enough to post a review on Amazon. Reviews really do make all the difference to authors and it is great to get feedback from you, the reader.

If this is the first of my novels you've read, you may be interested in the other Sgt Major Crane books, following Tom Crane and DI Anderson as they take on the worst crimes committed in and around Aldershot Garrison. At the time of writing there are eight Sgt Major Crane crime thrillers. In order, they are: Steps to Heaven, 40 Days 40 Nights, Honour Bound, Cordon of Lies, Regenerate, Hijack, Glass Cutter and Solid Proof.

Past Judgment is the first in a new series. It is a spin-off from the Sgt Major Crane novels and features Emma Harrison from Hijack and Sgt Billy Williams of the Special Investigations Branch of the Royal Military Police. The second book, Mortal Judgment and the third, Joint Judgement have just been released. Look out for more adventures from Billy and Emma in the Judgment series in the near future.

This book, Death Elements, is the second in the Crane and Anderson series.

All my books are available on Amazon.

You can keep in touch through my website http://www.wendycartmell.webs.com. I'm also on Twitter @wendycartmell.

Printed in Great Britain
by Amazon